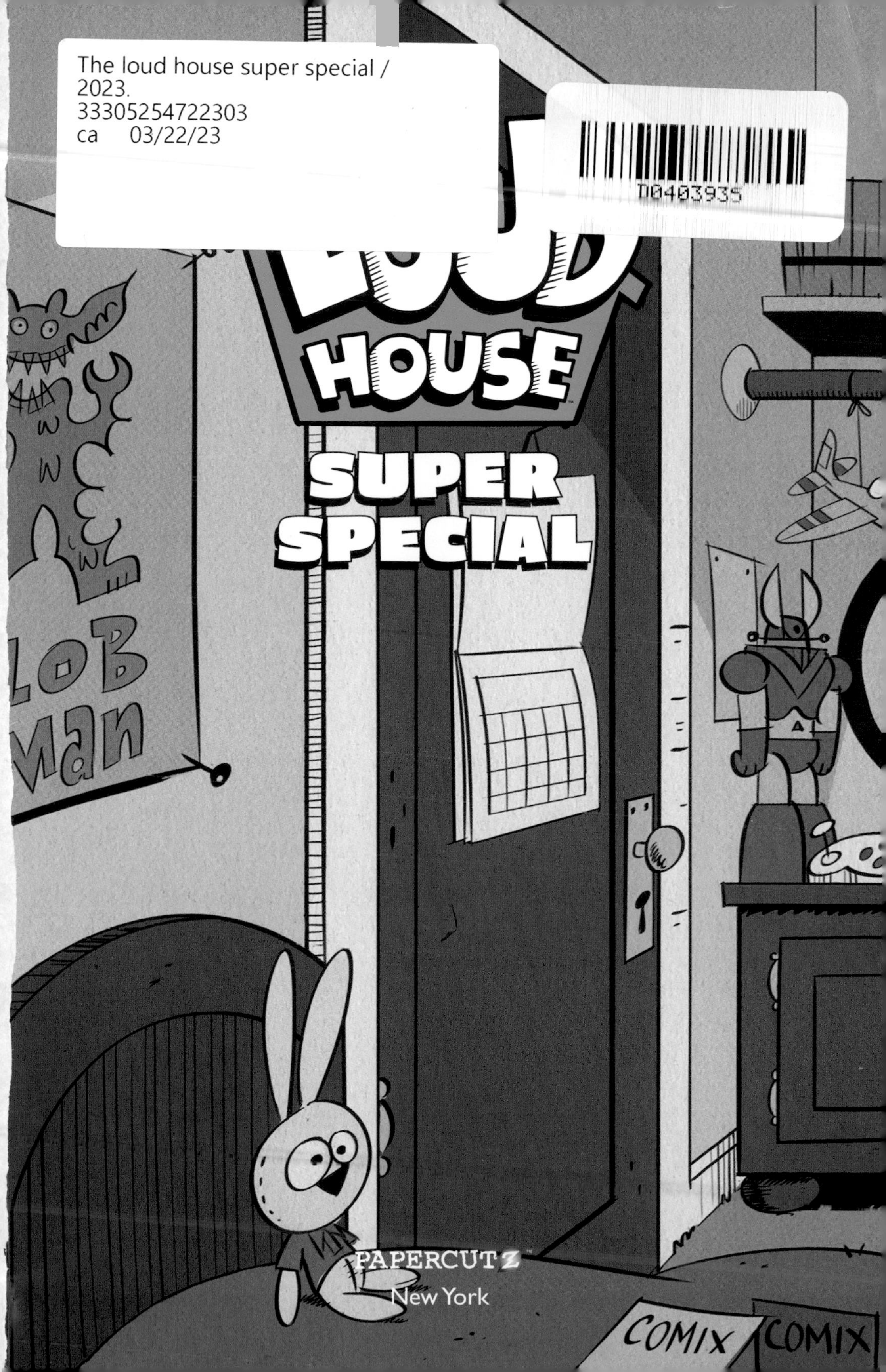
COMIX
COMIX

LOUD HOUSE
SUPER SPECIAL

PAPERCUTZ
New York

THE LOUD HOUSE
SUPER SPECIAL

“SUPER SPECIAL”

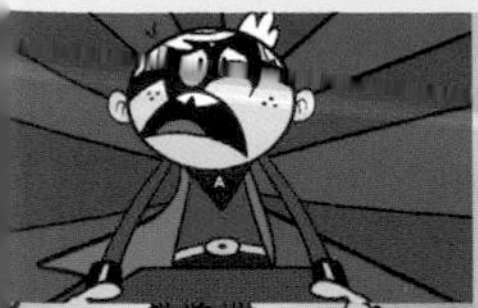

“UNDER-THE-FRONT-COVER OPERATION”
Erik Steinman — Writer
Izzy Boyce-Blanchard — Artist, Colorist
Wilson Ramos Jr. — Letterer

“SCENE PARTNER”
Erik Steinman — Writer
Zazo Aguiar — Artist, Colorist
Wilson Ramos Jr. — Letterer

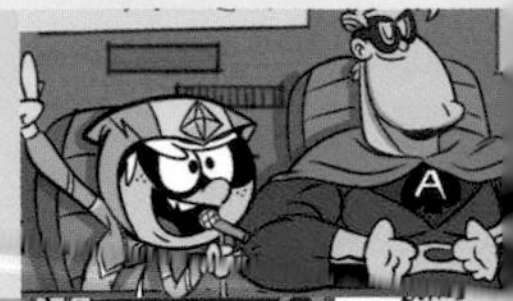

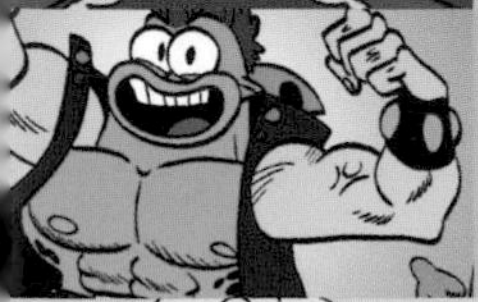

“NECESSARY EVIL”
Erik Steinman — Writer
Ryan Jampole — Artist
Erin Rodriguez — Colorist
Wilson Ramos Jr. — Letterer

“SURPRISE MEET AND GREET!”
Kacey Huang-Wooley — Writer
Lex Hobson — Artist, Colorist
Wilson Ramos Jr. — Letterer

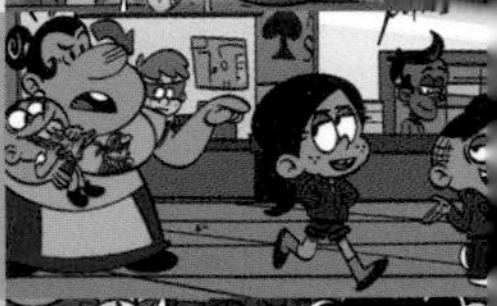

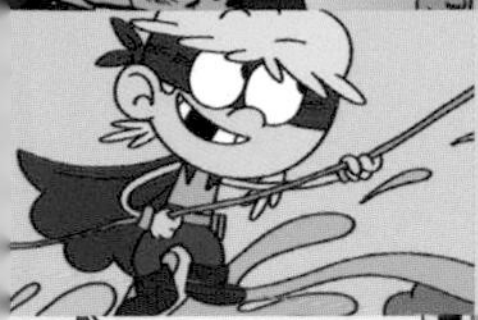

“A FELINE IN NEED”
Amanda Lioi — Writer, Artist, Colorist
Wilson Ramos Jr. — Letterer

“COMICS, TRICKS, AND CARL AMISS!”
Kacey Huang-Wooley — Writer
Lex Hobson — Artist, Colorist
Wilson Ramos Jr. — Letterer

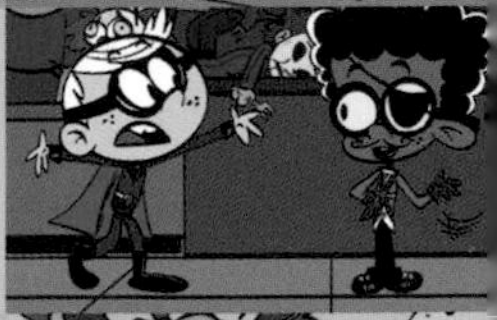

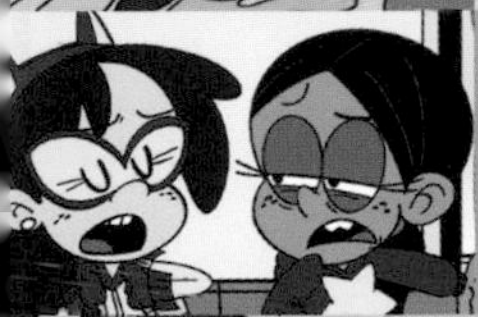

“CONVENTION CONFUSION”
Kiernan Sjursen-Lien — Writer
Erin Hyde — Artist, Colorist
Wilson Ramos Jr. — Letterer

“DRESSED TO POSE!”
Kacey Huang-Wooley — Writer
Lex Hobson — Artist, Colorist
Wilson Ramos Jr. — Letterer

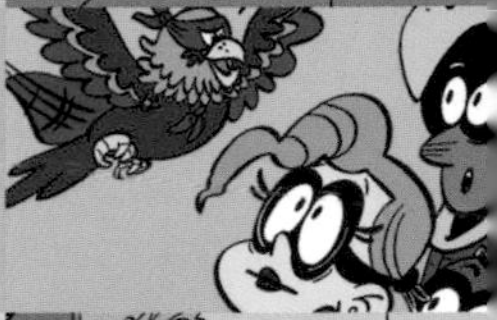

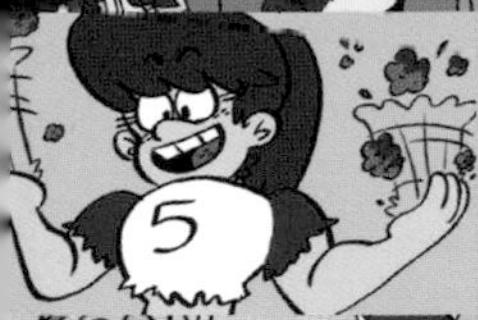
5

“SHREDDED BEEF”
Derek Fridolfs — Writer
Alexia Valentine — Artist
Ronaldo Barata — Colorist
Wilson Ramos Jr. — Letterer

“ACE SAVVY VS.... CARL?!”
Kacey Huang-Wooley — Writer
Lex Hobson — Artist, Colorist
Wilson Ramos Jr. — Letterer

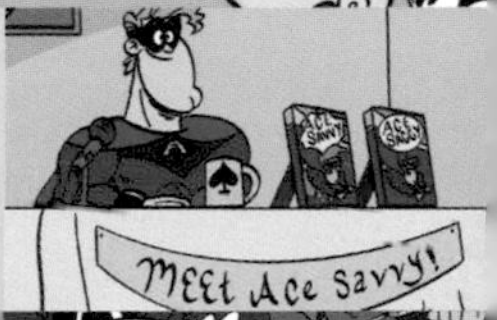
MEEt Ace Savvy!

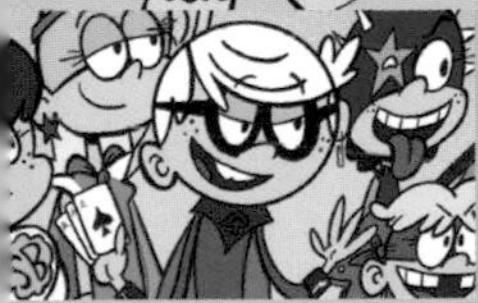

“THE CROWNED CAPER”
Kara and Amanda Fein — Writers
Chris Sabatino — Artist
Lex Hobson — Colorist
Wilson Ramos Jr. — Letterer

JOEL ZAMUDIO — Cover Artist

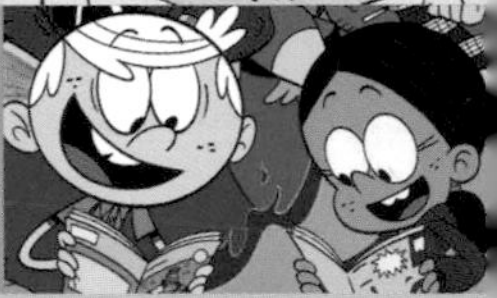

JAYJAY JACKSON — Design
KARLO ANTUNES, DANA CLUVERIUS, MOLLIE FREILICH, NEIL WADE, MIGUEL PUGA, LALO ALCARAZ, JOAN HILTY, KRISTEN YU-UM, EMILIE CRUZ, and ARTHUR “DJ” DESIN— Special Thanks
STEPHANIE BROOKS — Editor
JEFF WHITMAN — Comics Editor/Nickelodeon
MICOL HIATT — Comics Designer/Nickelodeon
JIM SALICRUP
Editor-in-Chief

ISBN: 978-1-5458-1024-8 paperback edition
ISBN: 978-1-5458-1023-1 hardcover edition

www.papercutz.com

Printed in China
February 2023

First Printing

MEET THE LOUD FAMILY *and friends!*

LINCOLN LOUD
THE MIDDLE CHILD

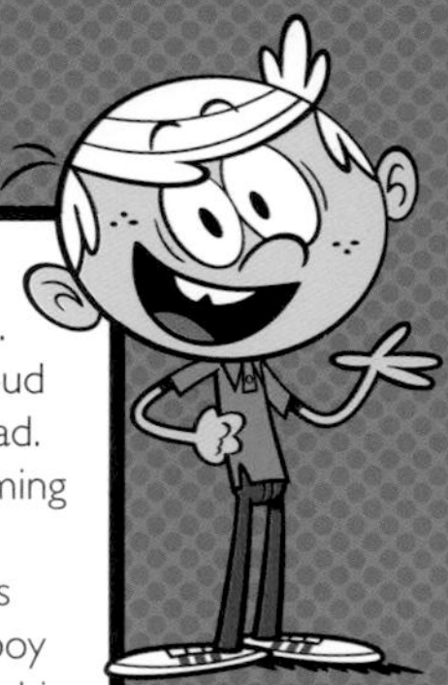

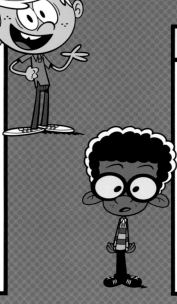

Lincoln is the middle child, with five older sisters and five younger sisters. He has learned that surviving the Loud household means staying a step ahead. He's the man with a plan, always coming up with a way to get what he wants or deal with a problem, even if things inevitably go wrong. Being the only boy comes with some perks. Lincoln gets his own room – even if it's just a converted linen closet. On the other hand, being the only boy also means he sometimes gets a little too much attention from his sisters. They mother him, tease him, and use him as the occasional lab rat or fashion show participant. Lincoln's sisters may drive him crazy, but he loves them and is always willing to help out if they need him.

CLYDE McBRIDE
THE BEST FRIEND

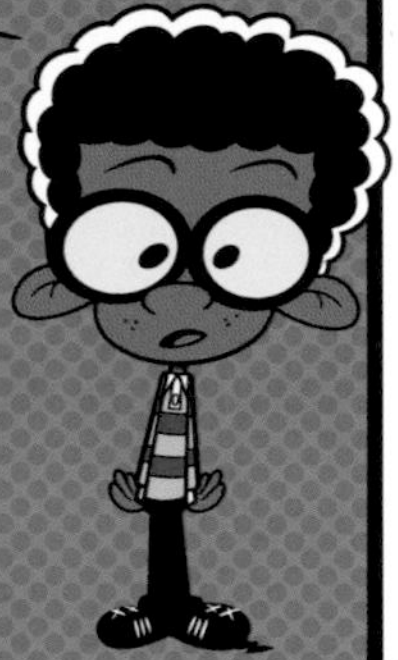

Clyde is Lincoln's partner in crime. He's always willing to go along with Lincoln's crazy schemes (even if he sees the flaws in them up-front). Lincoln and Clyde are two peas in a pod and share pretty much all of the same tastes in movies, comics, TV shows, toys – you name it. As an only child, Clyde envies Lincoln – how cool would it be to always have siblings around to talk to? But since Clyde spends so much time at the Loud household, he's almost an honorary sibling anyway.

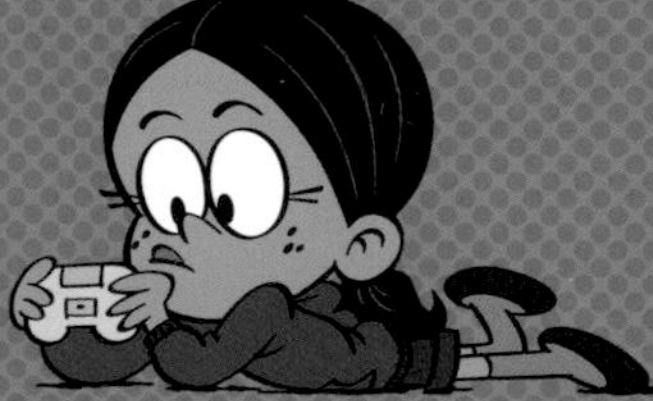

RONNIE ANNE SANTIAGO

Ronnie Anne's a skateboarding city girl now. She's fearless, free-spirited, and always quick to come up with a plan. She's one tough cookie, but she also has a sweet side. Ronnie Anne loves helping her family, and that's taught her to help others, too. When she's not pitching in at the family *mercado*, you can find her exploring the neighborhood with her best friend Sid, or ordering hot dogs with her skater buds Casey, Nikki, and Sameer.

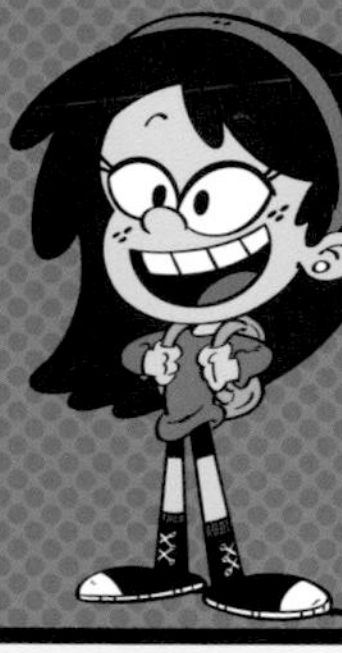

SID CHANG

Sid is Ronnie Anne's quirky best friend. She's new to the city but dives headfirst into everything she finds interesting. She and her family just moved into the apartment one floor above the Casagrandes. In fact, Sid's bedroom is right above Ronnie Anne's. A dream come true for any BFFs.

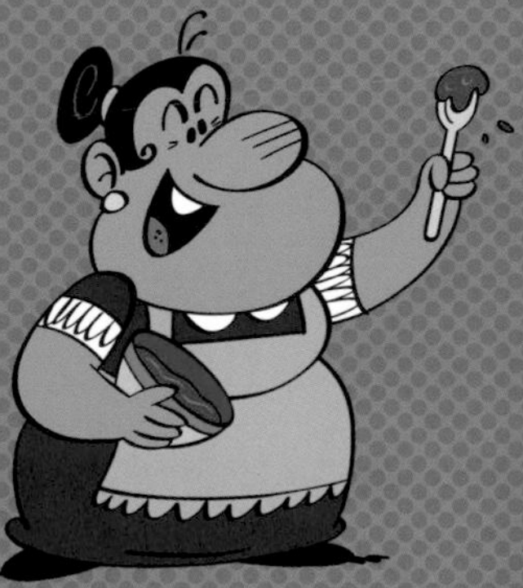

ROSA CASAGRANDE

Rosa is Carlos and Maria's mom and the *abuela* of the family (that means grandma)! She's the head of the household, the wisest Casagrande, and the master cook with a superhuman ability to tell when anyone in the house is hungry. She often tries to fix problems or illnesses with traditional Mexican home remedies and potions. She's very protective of her family… sometimes a little too much.

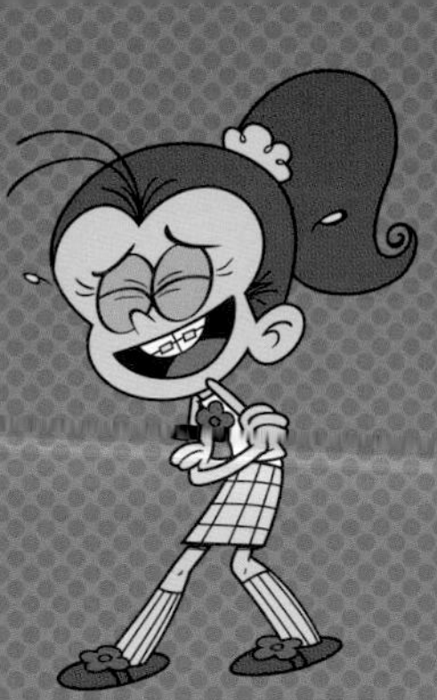

LUAN LOUD
THE JOKESTER

Luan's a standup comedienne who provides a nonstop barrage of silly puns. She's big on prop comedy too – squirting flowers and whoopee cushions – so you have to be on your toes whenever she's around. She loves to pull pranks and is a really good ventriloquist – she is often found doing bits with her dummy, Mr. Coconuts. Luan never lets anything get her down; to her, laughter IS the best medicine.

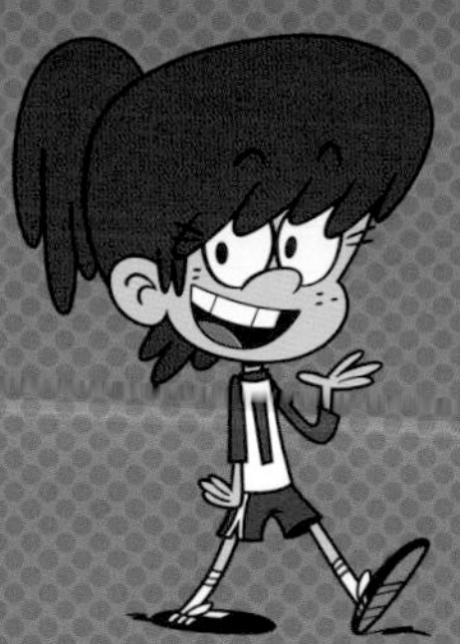

LYNN LOUD
THE ATHLETE

Lynn is athletic and full of energy and is always looking for a teammate. With her, it's all sports all the time. She'll turn anything into a sport. Putting away eggs? Jump shot! Score! Cleaning up the eggs? Slap shot! Score! Lynn is very competitive, but despite her competitive nature, she always tries to just have a good time.

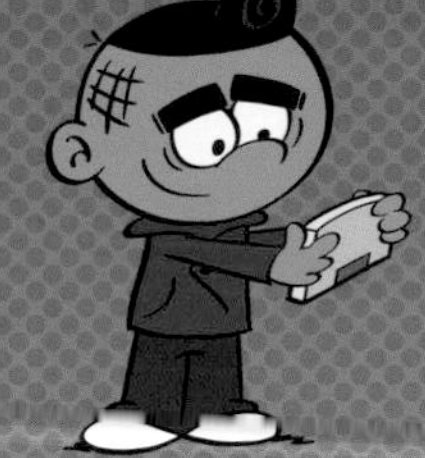

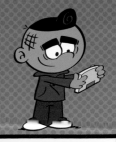

CARL CASAGRANDE

Carl is wise beyond his years. He's confident, outgoing, and puts a lot of time and effort into looking good. He likes to think of himself as a suave businessman and doesn't like to get caught playing with his action figures or wearing his footie PJs. Even though Bobby is nothing but nice to him, Carl sees his big cousin as his biggest rival.

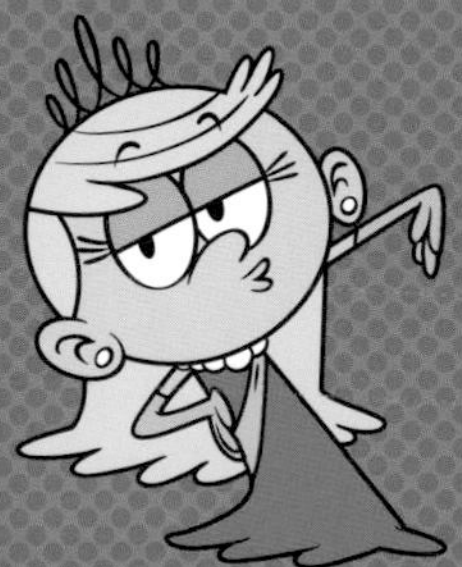

LOLA LOUD
THE BEAUTY QUEEN

Lola could not be more different from her twin sister, Lana. She's a pageant powerhouse whose interests include glitter, photo shoots, and her own beautiful, beautiful face. But don't let her cute, gap-toothed smile fool you; underneath all the sugar and spice lurks a Machiavellian mastermind. Whatever Lola wants, Lola gets – or else. She's the eyes and ears of the household and never resists an opportunity to tattle on troublemakers. But if you stay on Lola's good side, you've got yourself a fierce ally – and a lifetime supply of free makeovers.

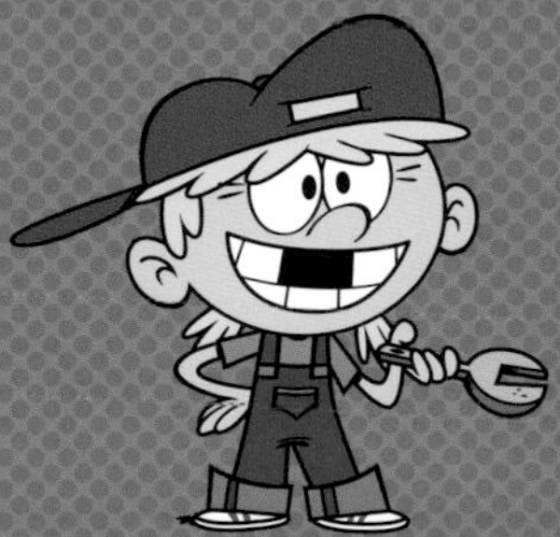

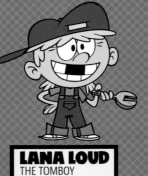

LANA LOUD
THE TOMBOY

Lana is the rough-and-tumble sparkplug counterpart to her twin sister, Lola. She's all about reptiles, mud pies, and muffler repair. She's the resident Ms. Fix-it and is always ready to lend a hand – the dirtier the job, the better. Need your toilet unclogged? Snake fed? Back-zit popped? Lana's your gal All she asks in return is a little A-B-C gum, or a handful of kibble (she often sneaks it from the dog bowl).

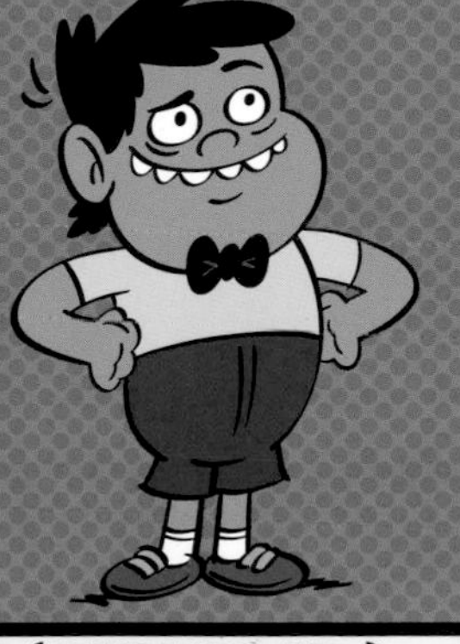

CJ (CARLOS JR.) CASAGRANDE

CJ is Carlota's younger brother and Carl and Carlitos' older brother. He was born with Down Syndrome. He lights up any room with his infectious smile and is always ready to play. He's obsessed with pirates and is BFFs with Bobby. He likes to wear a bowtie to any family occasion, and you can always catch him laughing or helping his *abuela*.

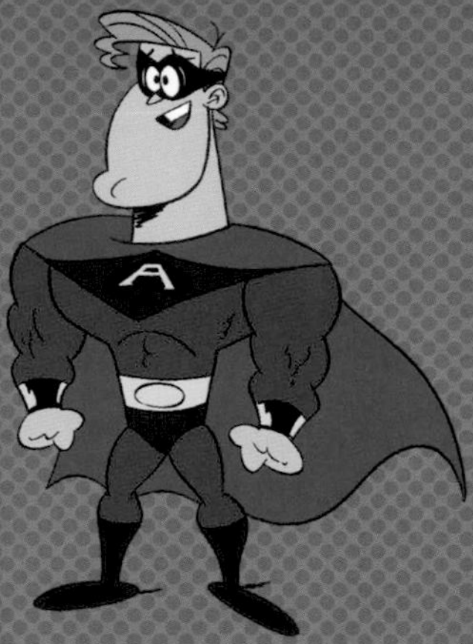

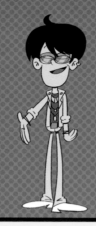

ACE SAVVY

A superhero character from a comicbook series that Lincoln is obsessed with and likes to cosplay as. Ace solves crimes and restores order in the world themed to a deck of cards and heavily loaded with card puns.

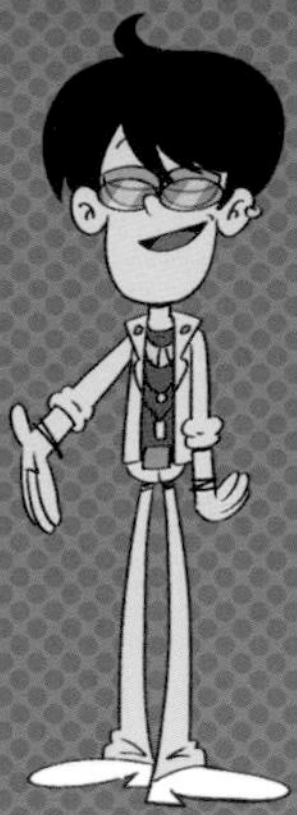

YOON KWAN

Yoon Kwan is the Korean American lead singer of the global K-pop sensation, "Twelve Is Midnight." He might not be the brightest bulb in the marquee but what he lacks in brains he makes up for in charm, smooth dance moves, and a sultry voice. He loves his fans and is known for being kind and approachable — through his music and charm, he makes everyone feel like his best friend.

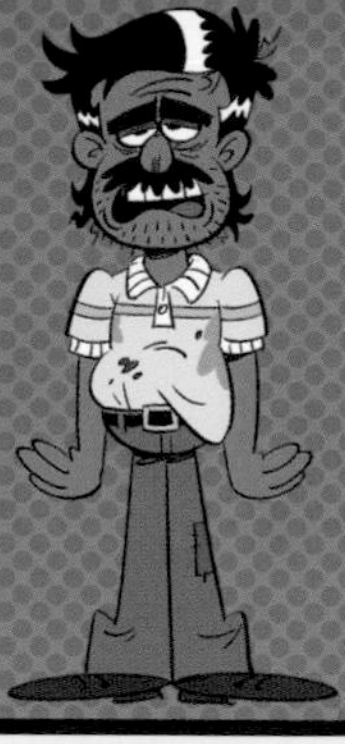

MR. BOLHOFNER

Mr. Bolhofner is Lincoln's gruff but well-meaning middle school teacher, whose stories of survival out in the wild are renowned throughout Royal Woods. He has a passion for smoked jerky and taxidermy, and a flair for playing the bass drum. He has two fierce pets that usually cause trouble at school: a piranha named Hank and a bobcat named Rocket. Although school rumors suggest that Bolhofner is scary enough to warrant the nickname "Skullhofner," Lincoln and his friends know that there's a big softie underneath his hard exterior.

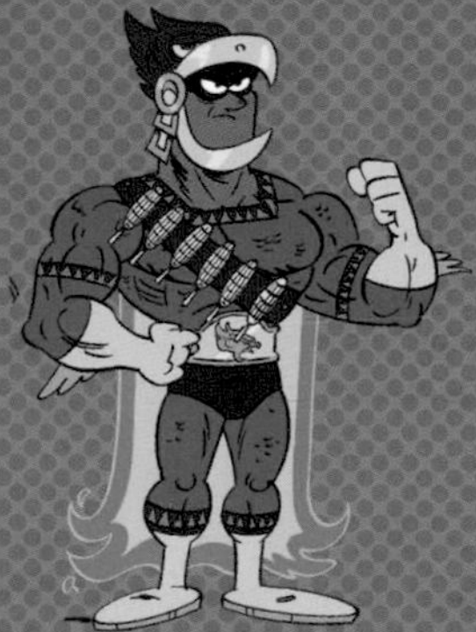

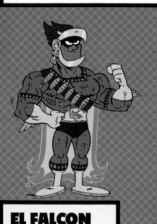

EL FALCON

El Falcon is Carl's favorite comicbook and cartoon hero. Residing in the Falcon Fortress, El Falcon is always ready to save the day by defeating his known enemies — the dastardly El Dragon and La Cobra. He relies not only on his super strength and ability to fly, but his iconic elote blaster and signature move, the elote chop! El Falcon always makes sure to do the right thing and stand up for those in need.

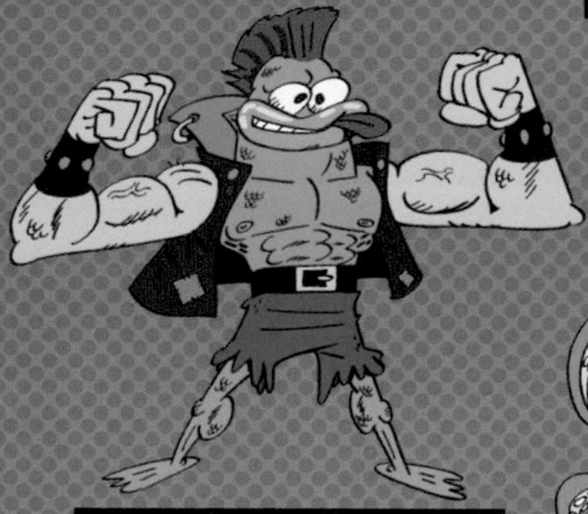

MUSCLE FISH

A beloved toy, video game and comicbook character in the Loud House universe. Muscle fish is a good natured, yet overzealous superhero getting himself into trouble by being "too extreme" when solving problems.

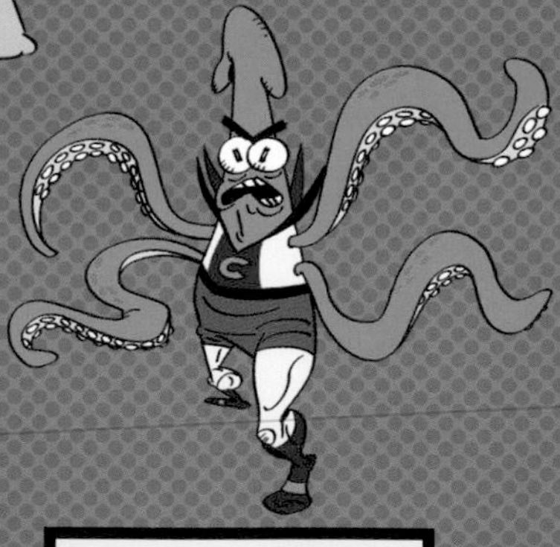

CEPHALOPLEX

An evil octopus-like villain who is determined to cause chaos, especially for the superhero Muscle Fish.

"UNDER-THE-FRONT-COVER OPERATION"

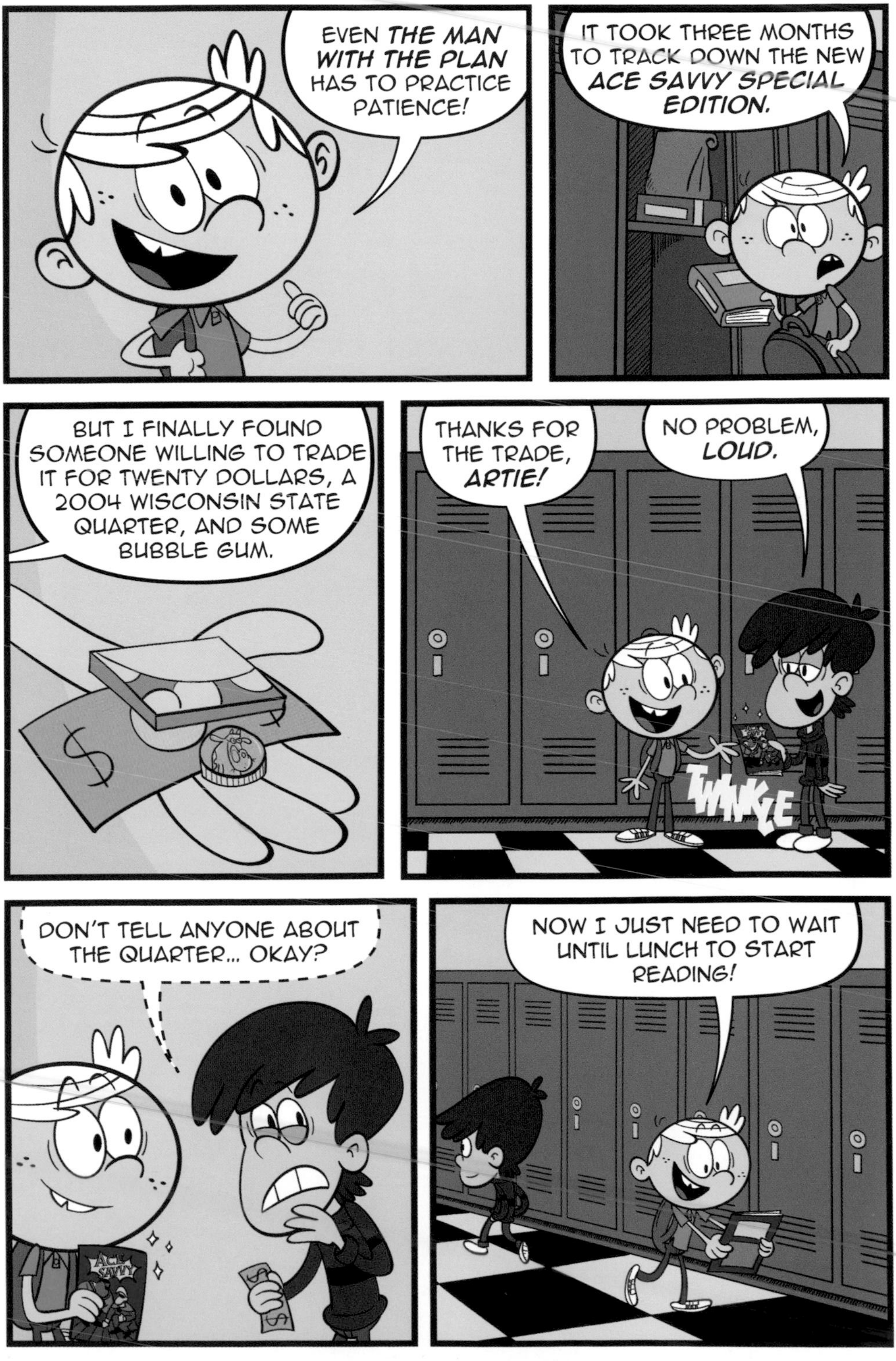

EVEN THE MAN WITH THE PLAN HAS TO PRACTICE PATIENCE!
IT TOOK THREE MONTHS TO TRACK DOWN THE NEW ACE SAVVY SPECIAL EDITION.
BUT I FINALLY FOUND SOMEONE WILLING TO TRADE IT FOR TWENTY DOLLARS, A 2004 WISCONSIN STATE QUARTER, AND SOME BUBBLE GUM.
THANKS FOR THE TRADE, ARTIE!
NO PROBLEM, LOUD.
TWINKLE
DON'T TELL ANYONE ABOUT THE QUARTER... OKAY?
ACE SAVVY
NOW I JUST NEED TO WAIT UNTIL LUNCH TO START READING!

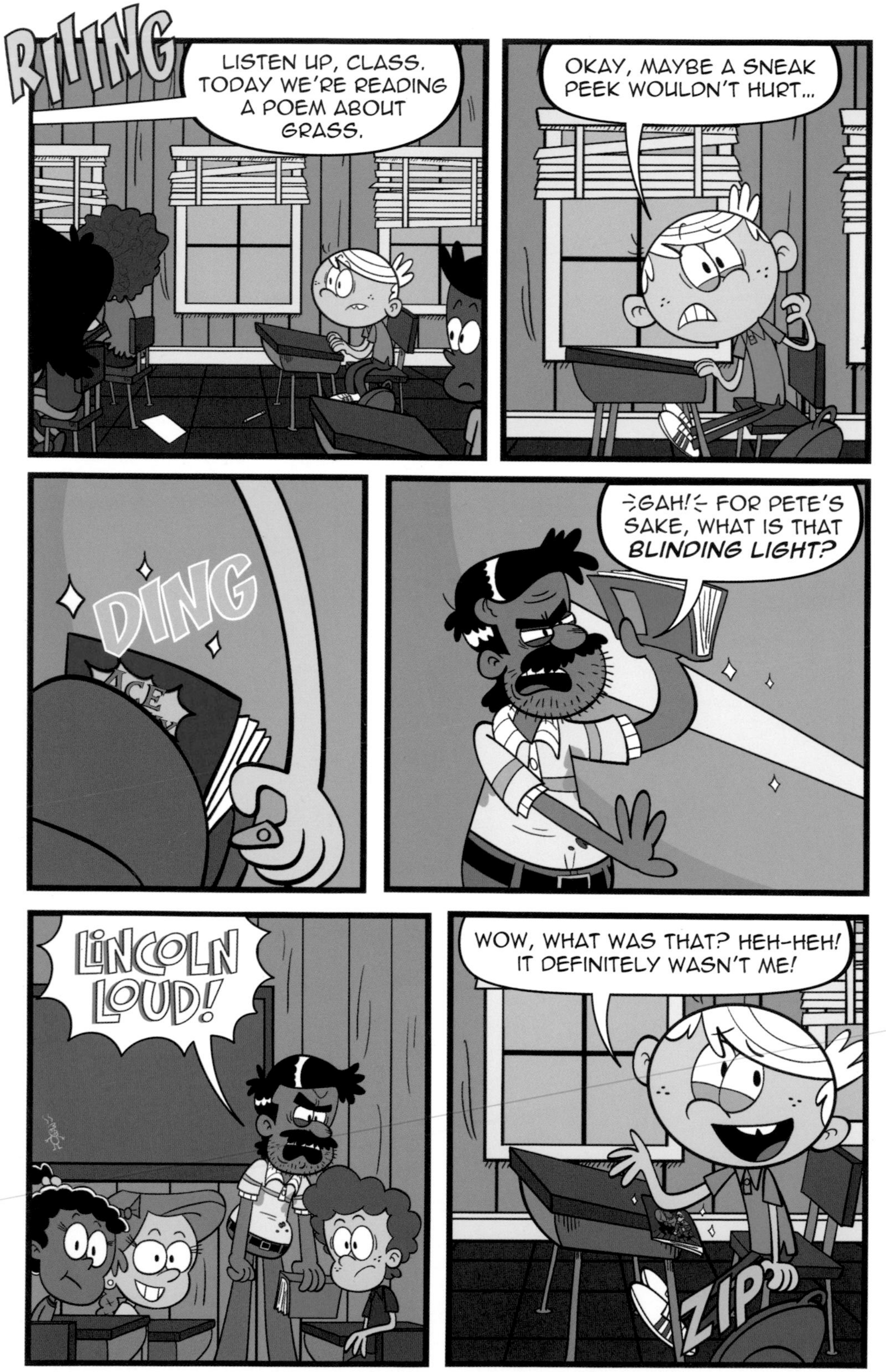
RIIING
LISTEN UP, CLASS. TODAY WE'RE READING A POEM ABOUT GRASS.
OKAY, MAYBE A SNEAK PEEK WOULDN'T HURT...
DING
GAH! FOR PETE'S SAKE, WHAT IS THAT BLINDING LIGHT?
LINCOLN LOUD!
WOW, WHAT WAS THAT? HEH-HEH! IT DEFINITELY WASN'T ME!
ZIP

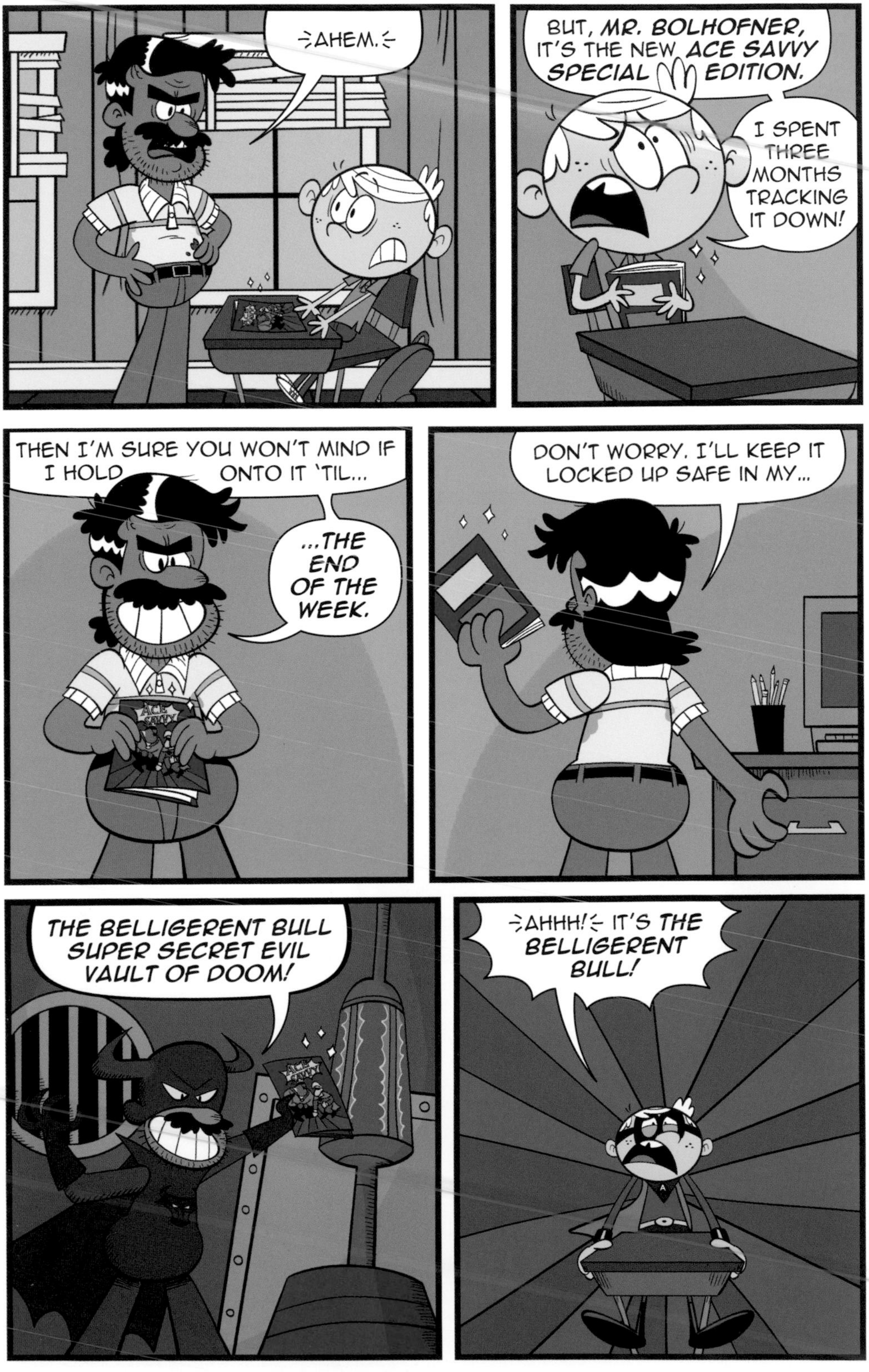
AHEM.
BUT, MR. BOLHOFNER, IT'S THE NEW ACE SAVVY SPECIAL EDITION.
I SPENT THREE MONTHS TRACKING IT DOWN!
THEN I'M SURE YOU WON'T MIND IF I HOLD ONTO IT 'TIL...
...THE END OF THE WEEK.
ACE SAVVY
DON'T WORRY. I'LL KEEP IT LOCKED UP SAFE IN MY...
THE BELLIGERENT BULL SUPER SECRET EVIL VAULT OF DOOM!
ACE SAVVY
AHHH! IT'S THE BELLIGERENT BULL!

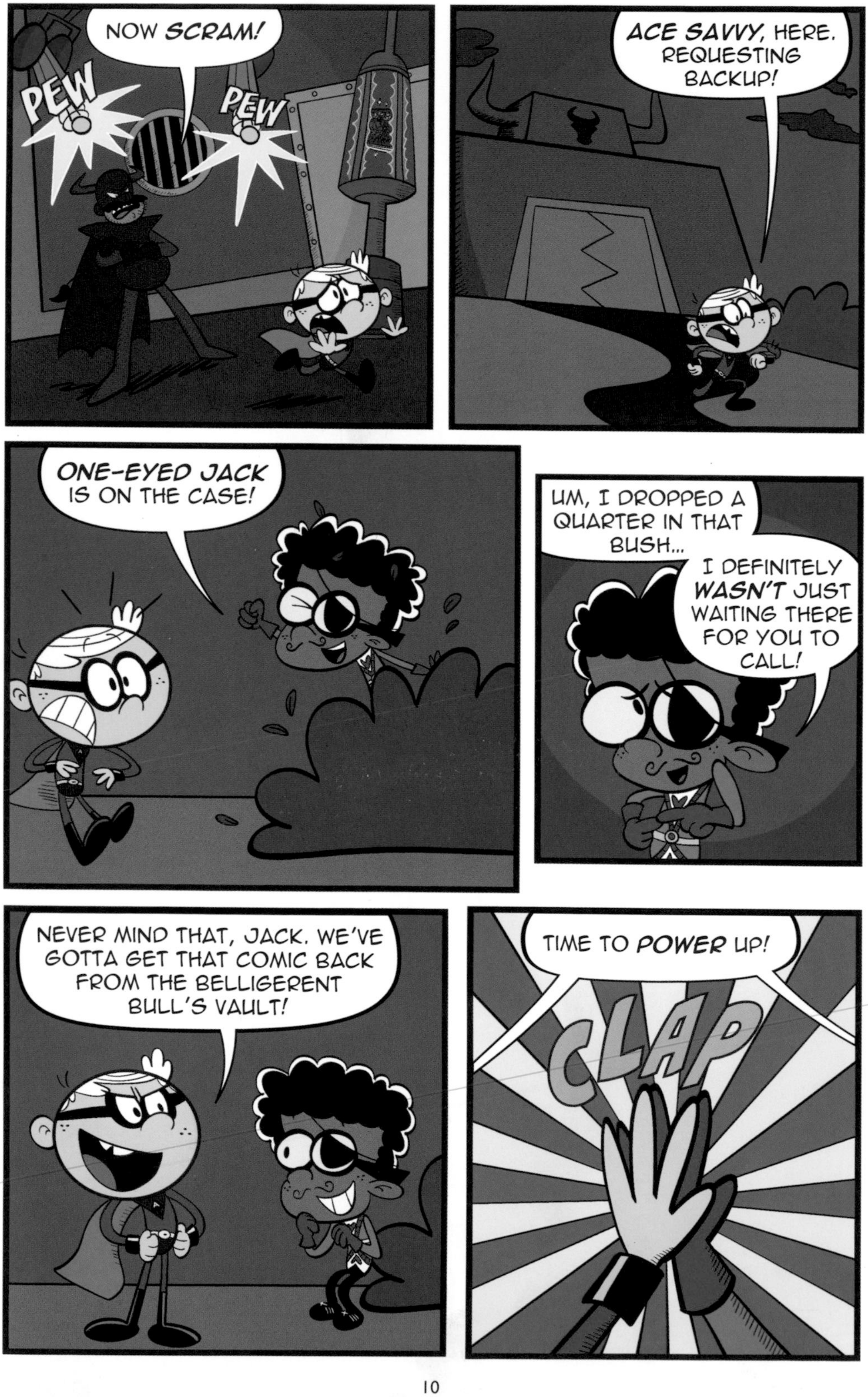
NOW SCRAM!
PEW
PEW
ACE SAVVY, HERE. REQUESTING BACKUP!
ONE-EYED JACK IS ON THE CASE!
UM, I DROPPED A QUARTER IN THAT BUSH...
I DEFINITELY WASN'T JUST WAITING THERE FOR YOU TO CALL!
NEVER MIND THAT, JACK. WE'VE GOTTA GET THAT COMIC BACK FROM THE BELLIGERENT BULL'S VAULT!
TIME TO POWER UP!
CLAP

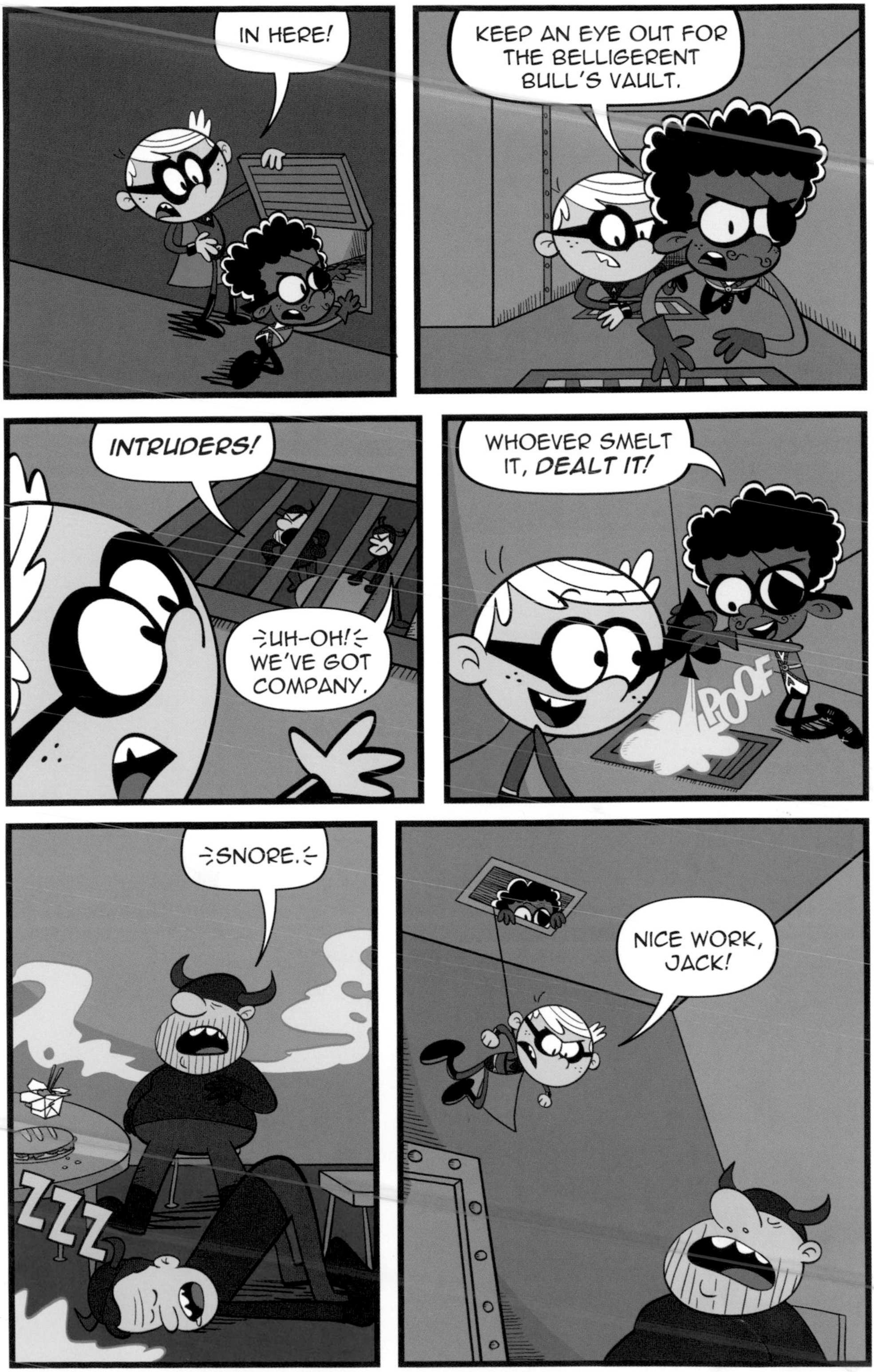
IN HERE!
KEEP AN EYE OUT FOR THE BELLIGERENT BULL'S VAULT.
INTRUDERS!
UH-OH! WE'VE GOT COMPANY.
WHOEVER SMELT IT, DEALT IT!
POOF
SNORE.
ZZZ
NICE WORK, JACK!

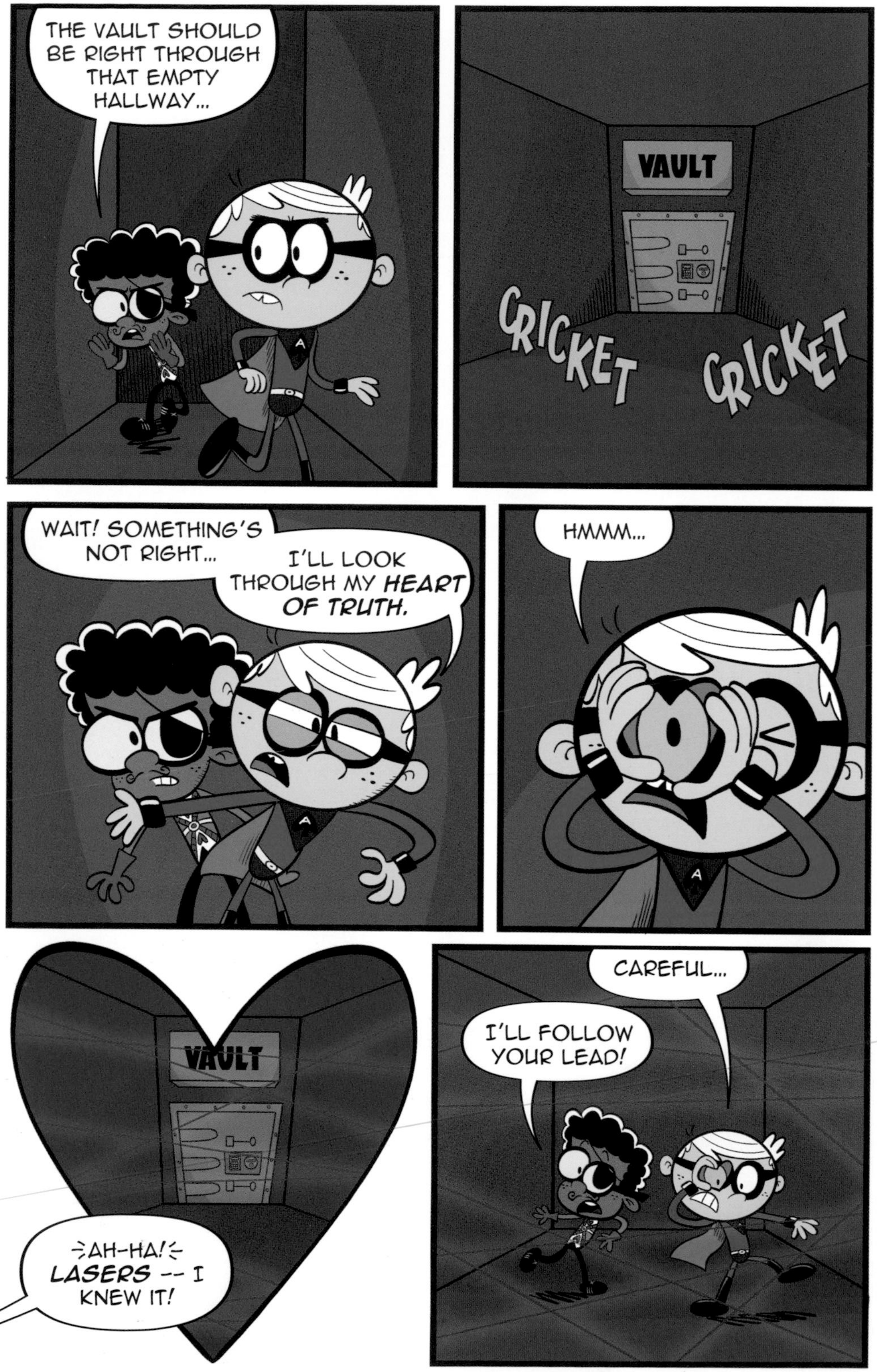
THE VAULT SHOULD BE RIGHT THROUGH THAT EMPTY HALLWAY...
VAULT
CRICKET
CRICKET
WAIT! SOMETHING'S NOT RIGHT...
I'LL LOOK THROUGH MY HEART OF TRUTH.
HMMM...
VAULT
AH-HA! LASERS -- I KNEW IT!
CAREFUL...
I'LL FOLLOW YOUR LEAD!

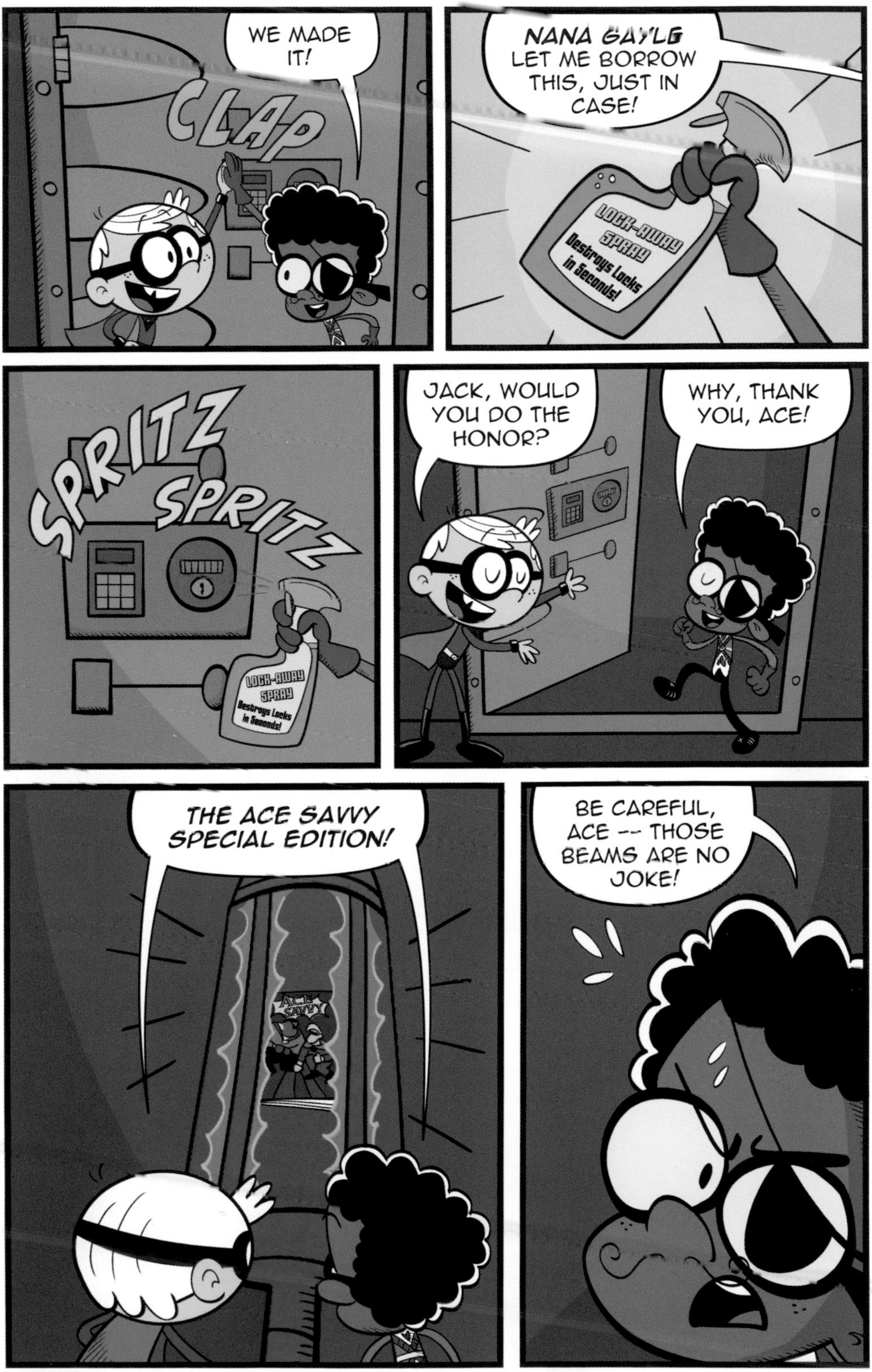
WE MADE IT!
CLAP
NANA GAYLE LET ME BORROW THIS, JUST IN CASE!
LOCK-AWAY SPRAY Destroys Locks in Seconds!
SPRITZ
SPRITZ
LOCK-AWAY SPRAY Destroys Locks in Seconds!
JACK, WOULD YOU DO THE HONOR?
WHY, THANK YOU, ACE!
THE ACE SAVVY SPECIAL EDITION!
ACE SAVVY
BE CAREFUL, ACE -- THOSE BEAMS ARE NO JOKE!

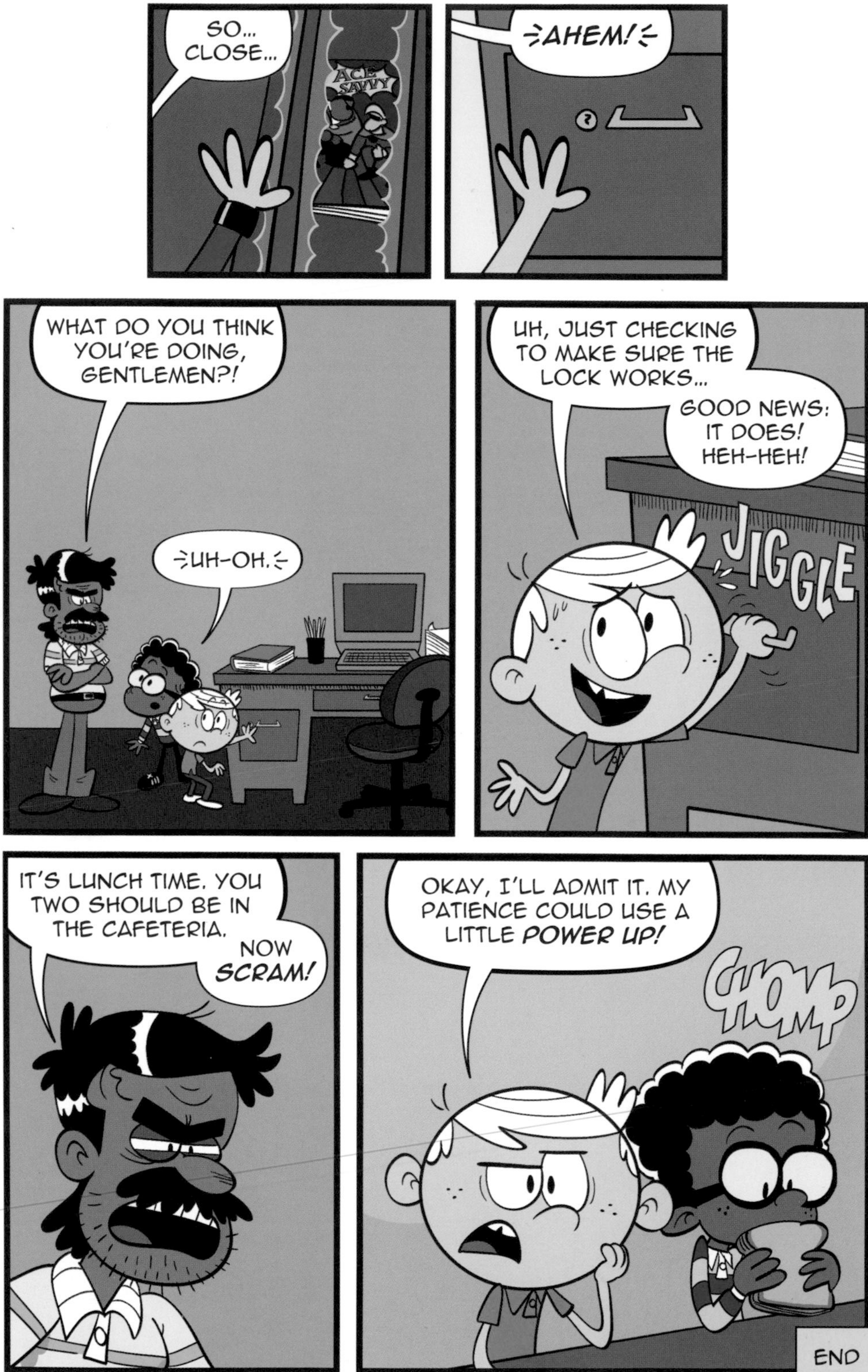
SO... CLOSE...
ACE SAVVY
AHEM!
WHAT DO YOU THINK YOU'RE DOING, GENTLEMEN?!
UH-OH.
UH, JUST CHECKING TO MAKE SURE THE LOCK WORKS...
GOOD NEWS: IT DOES! HEH-HEH!
JIGGLE
IT'S LUNCH TIME. YOU TWO SHOULD BE IN THE CAFETERIA.
NOW SCRAM!
OKAY, I'LL ADMIT IT. MY PATIENCE COULD USE A LITTLE POWER UP!
CHOMP
END

"NECESSARY EVIL"

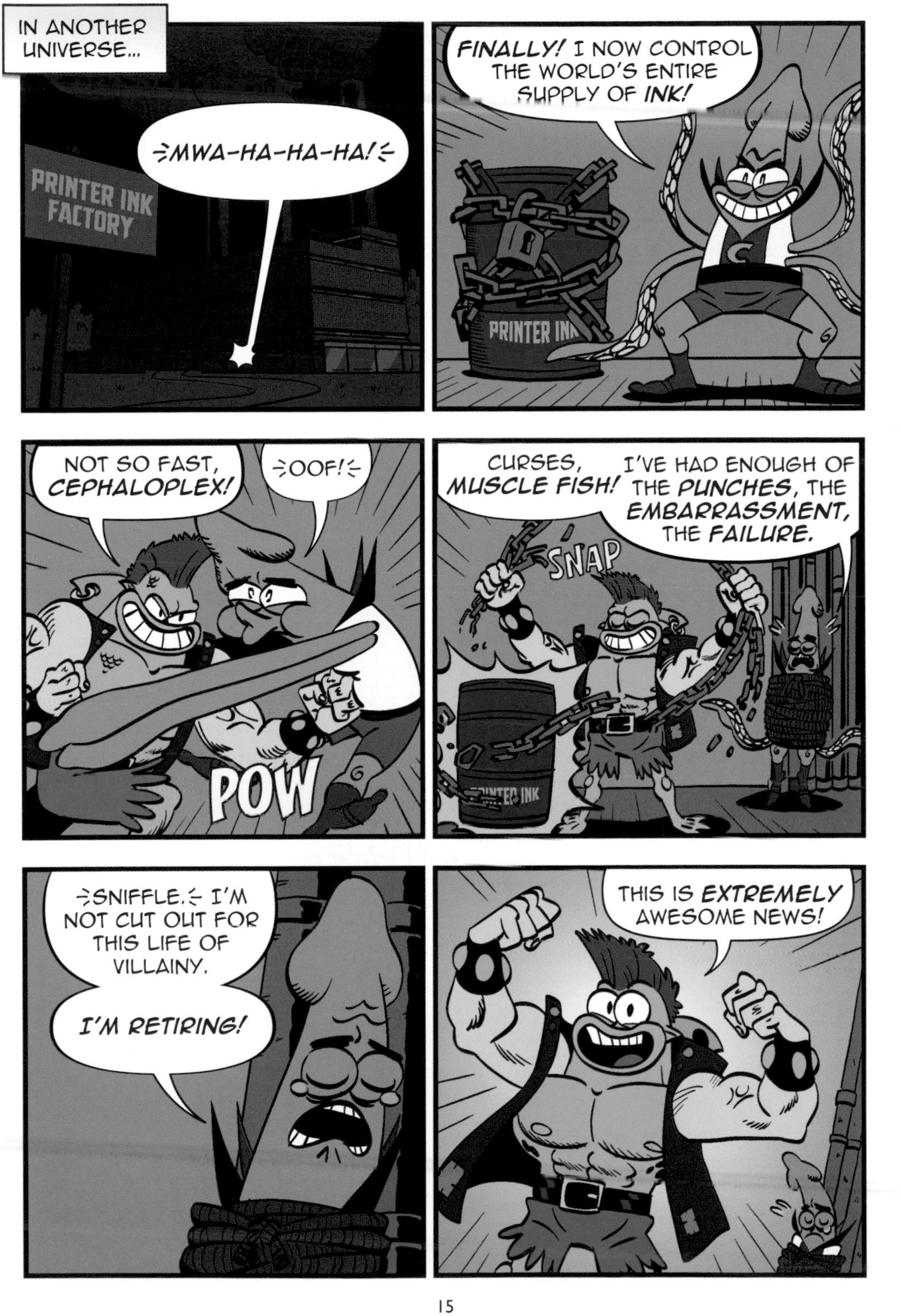
IN ANOTHER UNIVERSE...
PRINTER INK FACTORY
MWA-HA-HA-HA!
FINALLY! I NOW CONTROL THE WORLD'S ENTIRE SUPPLY OF INK!
PRINTER INK
NOT SO FAST, CEPHALOPLEX!
OOF!
POW
CURSES, MUSCLE FISH!
I'VE HAD ENOUGH OF THE PUNCHES, THE EMBARRASSMENT, THE FAILURE.
SNAP
SNIFFLE. I'M NOT CUT OUT FOR THIS LIFE OF VILLAINY.
I'M RETIRING!
THIS IS EXTREMELY AWESOME NEWS!

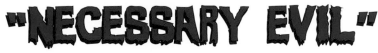

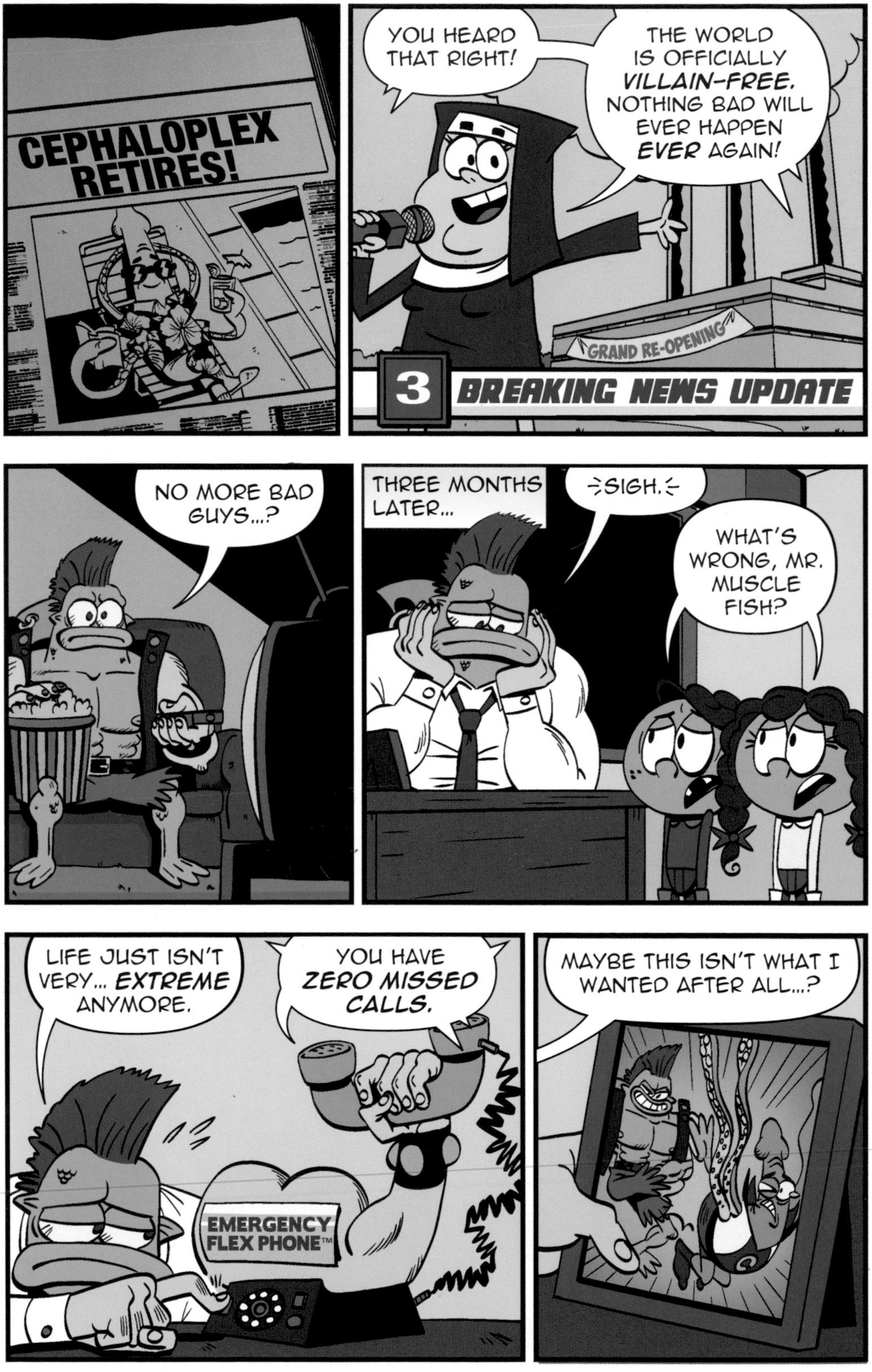
CEPHALOPLEX RETIRES!
YOU HEARD THAT RIGHT!
THE WORLD IS OFFICIALLY VILLAIN-FREE. NOTHING BAD WILL EVER HAPPEN EVER AGAIN!
GRAND RE-OPENING
3 BREAKING NEWS UPDATE
NO MORE BAD GUYS...?
THREE MONTHS LATER...
SIGH.
WHAT'S WRONG, MR. MUSCLE FISH?
LIFE JUST ISN'T VERY... EXTREME ANYMORE.
YOU HAVE ZERO MISSED CALLS.
EMERGENCY FLEX PHONE™
MAYBE THIS ISN'T WHAT I WANTED AFTER ALL...?

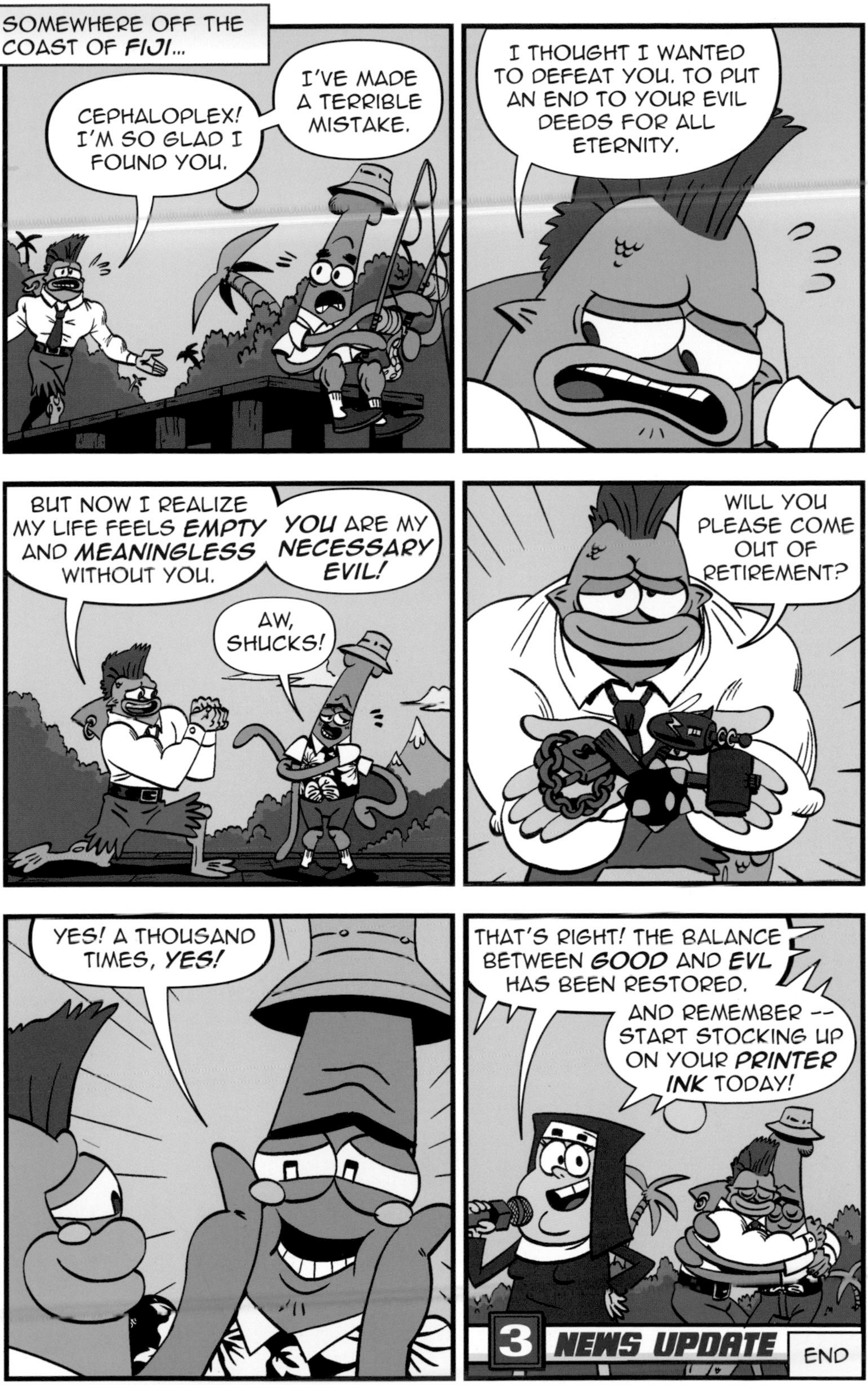
SOMEWHERE OFF THE COAST OF FIJI...
CEPHALOPLEX! I'M SO GLAD I FOUND YOU.
I'VE MADE A TERRIBLE MISTAKE.
I THOUGHT I WANTED TO DEFEAT YOU. TO PUT AN END TO YOUR EVIL DEEDS FOR ALL ETERNITY.
BUT NOW I REALIZE MY LIFE FEELS EMPTY AND MEANINGLESS WITHOUT YOU.
YOU ARE MY NECESSARY EVIL!
AW, SHUCKS!
WILL YOU PLEASE COME OUT OF RETIREMENT?
YES! A THOUSAND TIMES, YES!
THAT'S RIGHT! THE BALANCE BETWEEN GOOD AND EVL HAS BEEN RESTORED.
AND REMEMBER -- START STOCKING UP ON YOUR PRINTER INK TODAY!
3 NEWS UPDATE
END

"A FELINE IN NEED"

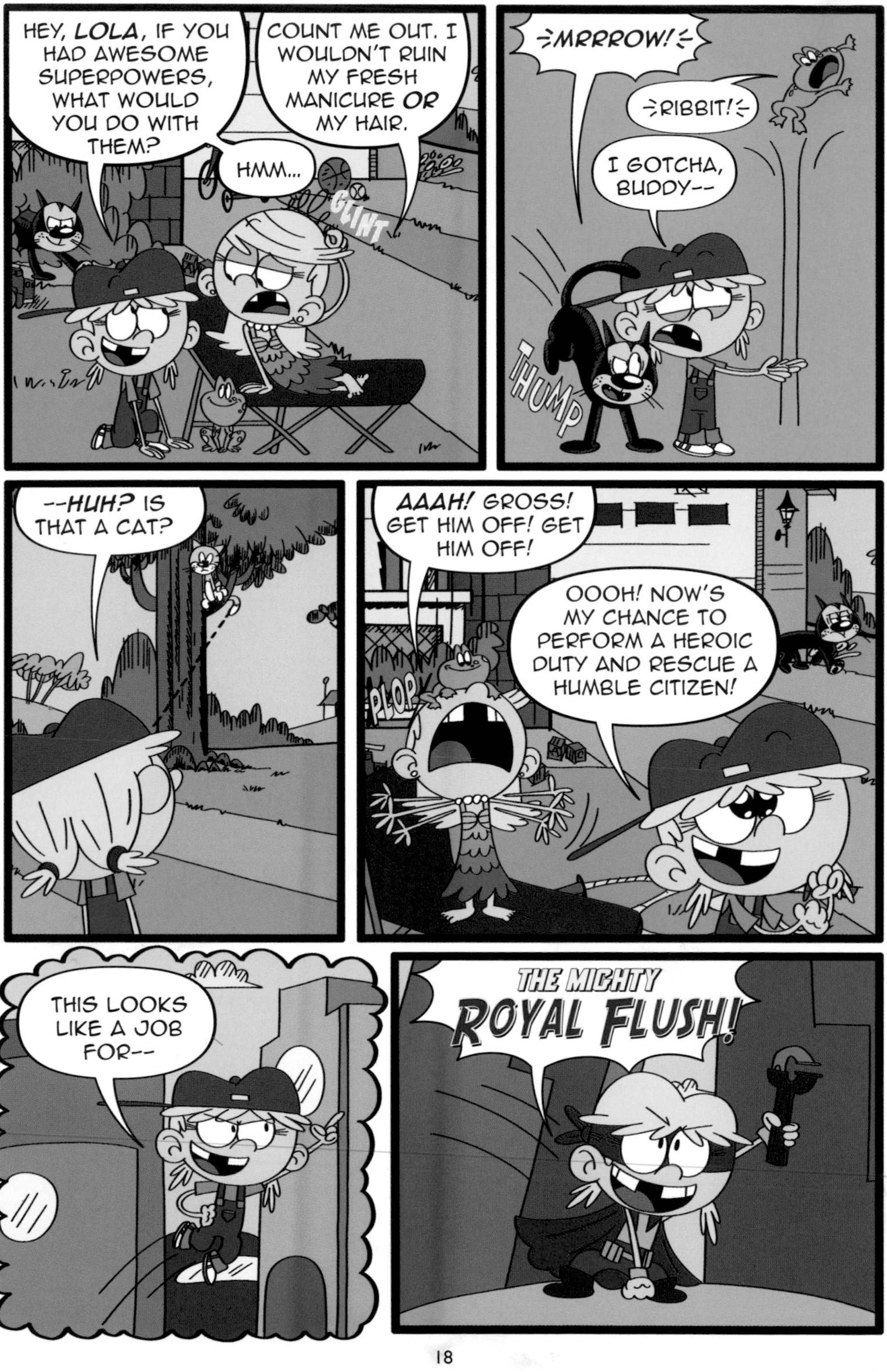
HEY, LOLA, IF YOU HAD AWESOME SUPERPOWERS, WHAT WOULD YOU DO WITH THEM?
HMM...
COUNT ME OUT. I WOULDN'T RUIN MY FRESH MANICURE OR MY HAIR.
GLINT
MRRROW!
RIBBIT!
I GOTCHA, BUDDY--
THUMP
--HUH? IS THAT A CAT?
AAAH! GROSS! GET HIM OFF! GET HIM OFF!
PLOP
OOOH! NOW'S MY CHANCE TO PERFORM A HEROIC DUTY AND RESCUE A HUMBLE CITIZEN!
THIS LOOKS LIKE A JOB FOR--
THE MIGHTY ROYAL FLUSH!

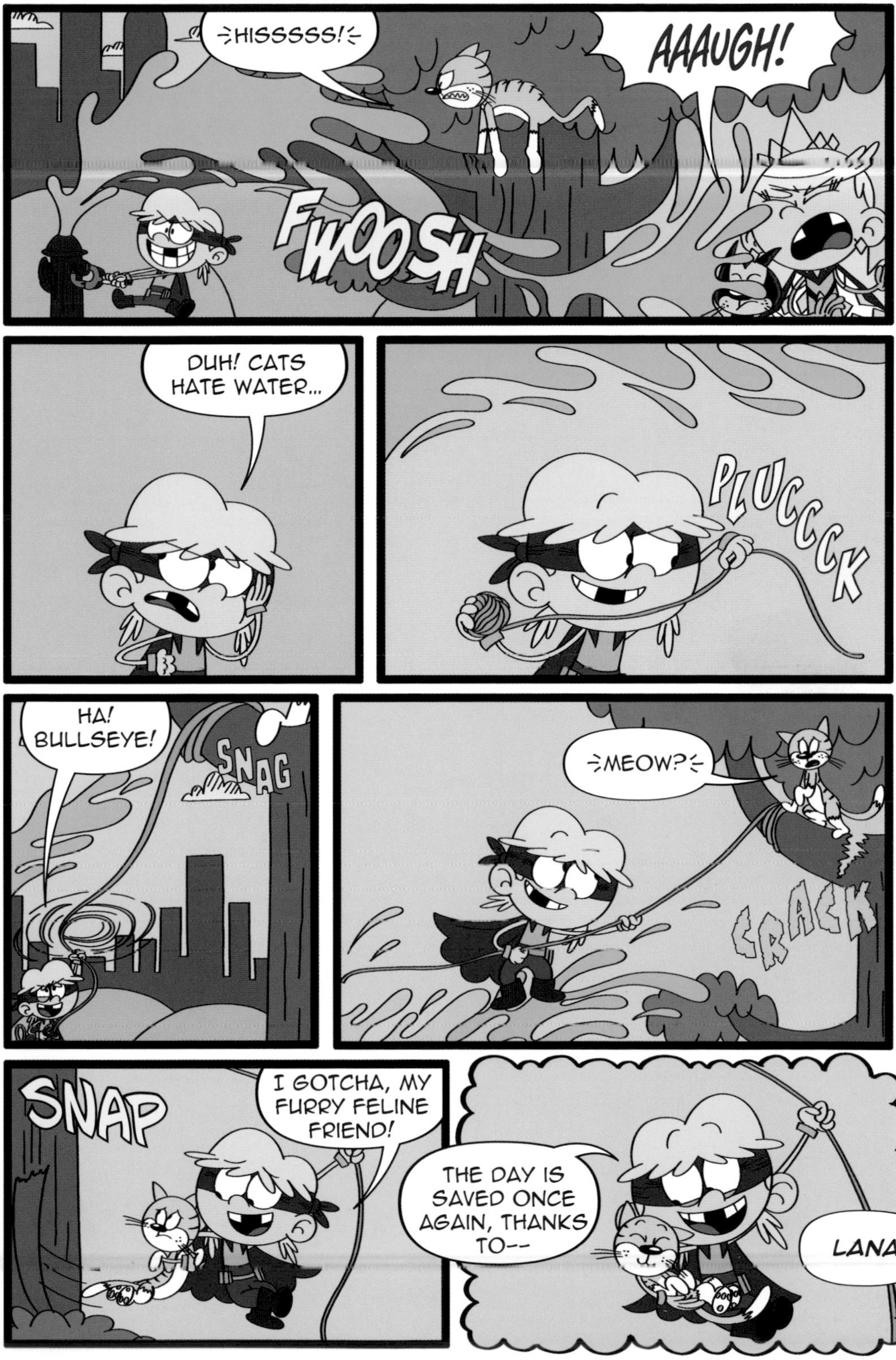
HISSSSS!
AAAUGH!
FWOOSH
DUH! CATS HATE WATER...
PLUCCCK
HA! BULLSEYE!
SNAG
MEOW?
CRACK
SNAP
I GOTCHA, MY FURRY FELINE FRIEND!
THE DAY IS SAVED ONCE AGAIN, THANKS TO--
LANA!

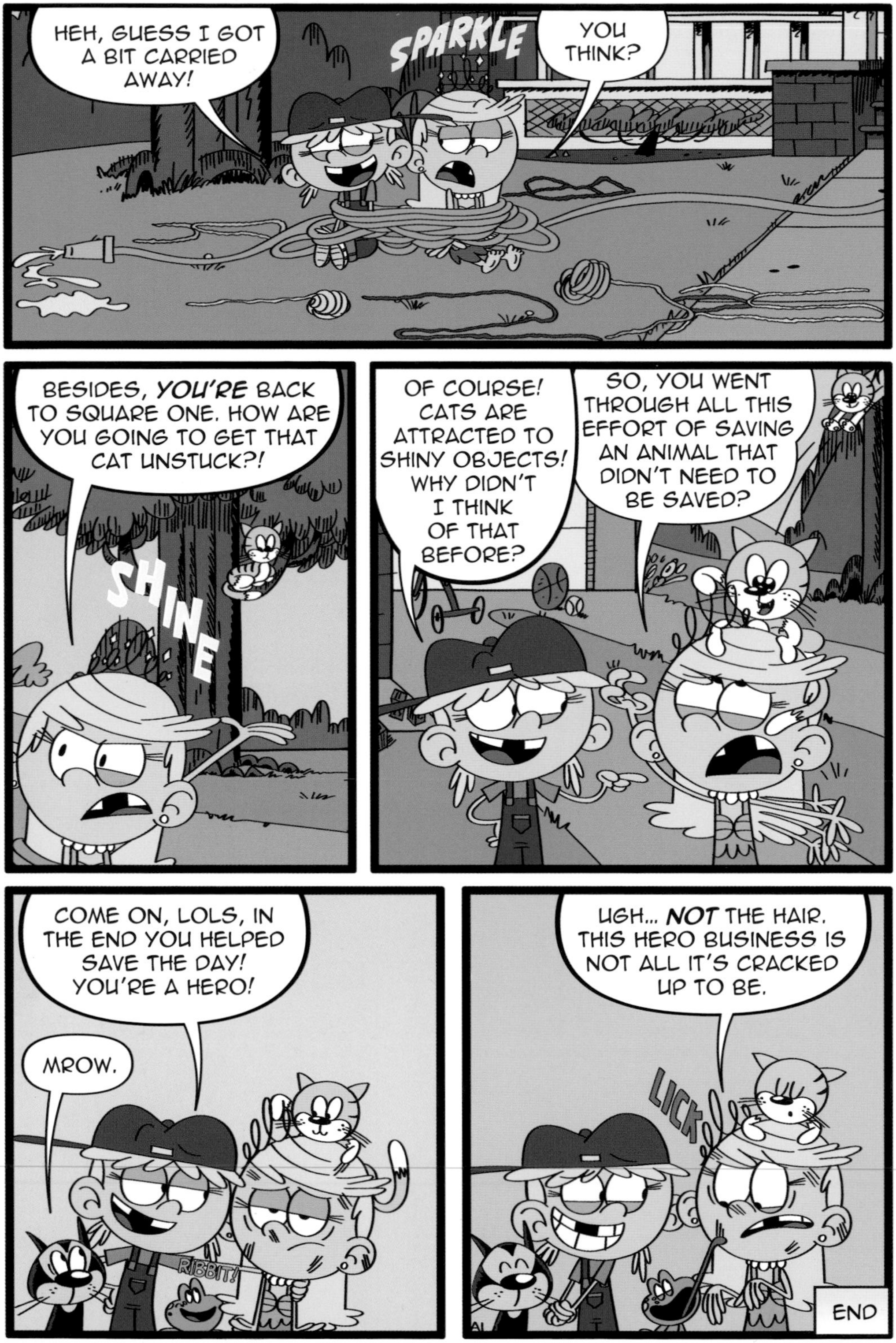
HEH, GUESS I GOT A BIT CARRIED AWAY!
SPARKLE
YOU THINK?
BESIDES, *YOU'RE* BACK TO SQUARE ONE. HOW ARE YOU GOING TO GET THAT CAT UNSTUCK?!
SHINE
OF COURSE! CATS ARE ATTRACTED TO SHINY OBJECTS! WHY DIDN'T I THINK OF THAT BEFORE?
SO, YOU WENT THROUGH ALL THIS EFFORT OF SAVING AN ANIMAL THAT DIDN'T NEED TO BE SAVED?
COME ON, LOLS, IN THE END YOU HELPED SAVE THE DAY! YOU'RE A HERO!
MROW.
RIBBIT!
UGH... ***NOT*** THE HAIR. THIS HERO BUSINESS IS NOT ALL IT'S CRACKED UP TO BE.
LICK
END

"CONVENTION CONFUSION"

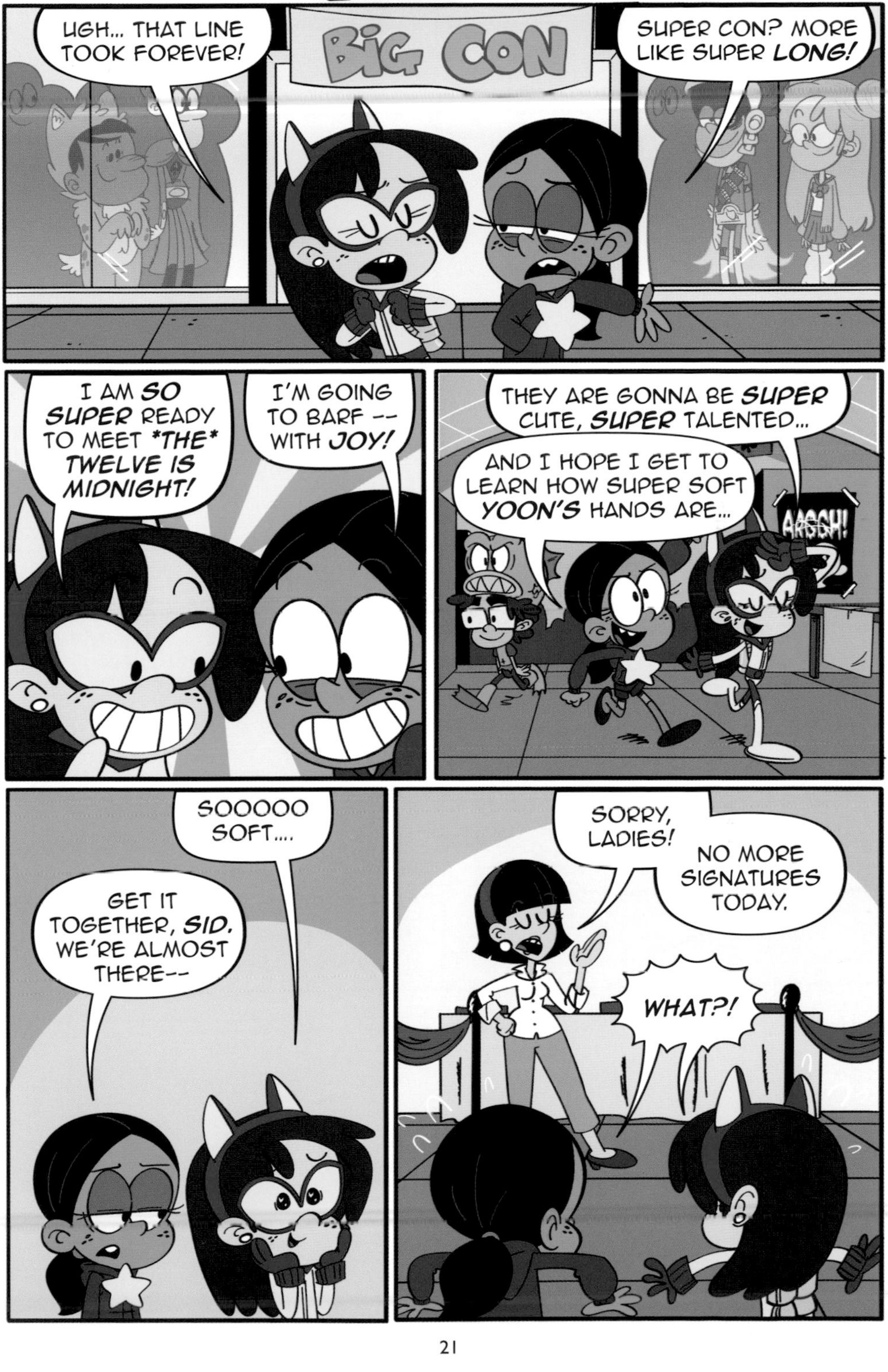
BIG CON
UGH... THAT LINE TOOK FOREVER!
SUPER CON? MORE LIKE SUPER LONG!
I AM SO SUPER READY TO MEET *THE* TWELVE IS MIDNIGHT!
I'M GOING TO BARF -- WITH JOY!
THEY ARE GONNA BE SUPER CUTE, SUPER TALENTED...
AND I HOPE I GET TO LEARN HOW SUPER SOFT YOON'S HANDS ARE...
ARGGH!
SOOOOO SOFT....
GET IT TOGETHER, SID. WE'RE ALMOST THERE--
SORRY, LADIES!
NO MORE SIGNATURES TODAY.
WHAT?!

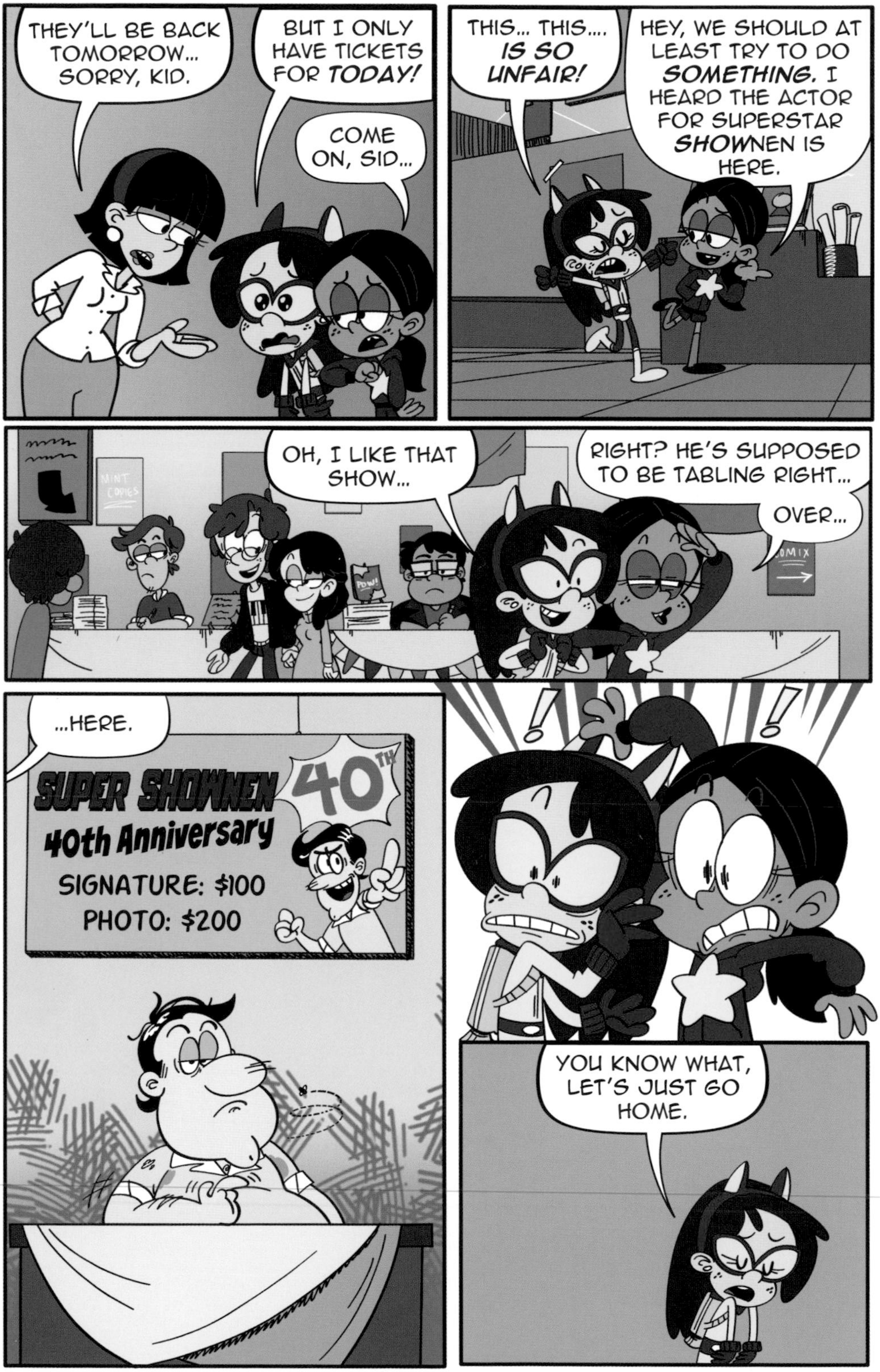
THEY'LL BE BACK TOMORROW... SORRY, KID.
BUT I ONLY HAVE TICKETS FOR *TODAY!*
COME ON, SID...
THIS... THIS.... *IS SO UNFAIR!*
HEY, WE SHOULD AT LEAST TRY TO DO *SOMETHING.* I HEARD THE ACTOR FOR SUPERSTAR *SHOW*NEN IS HERE.
MINT COPIES
OH, I LIKE THAT SHOW...
RIGHT? HE'S SUPPOSED TO BE TABLING RIGHT...
OVER...
POW!
COMIX
...HERE.
SUPER SHOWNEN
40TH
40th Anniversary
SIGNATURE: $100
PHOTO: $200
!
!
YOU KNOW WHAT, LET'S JUST GO HOME.

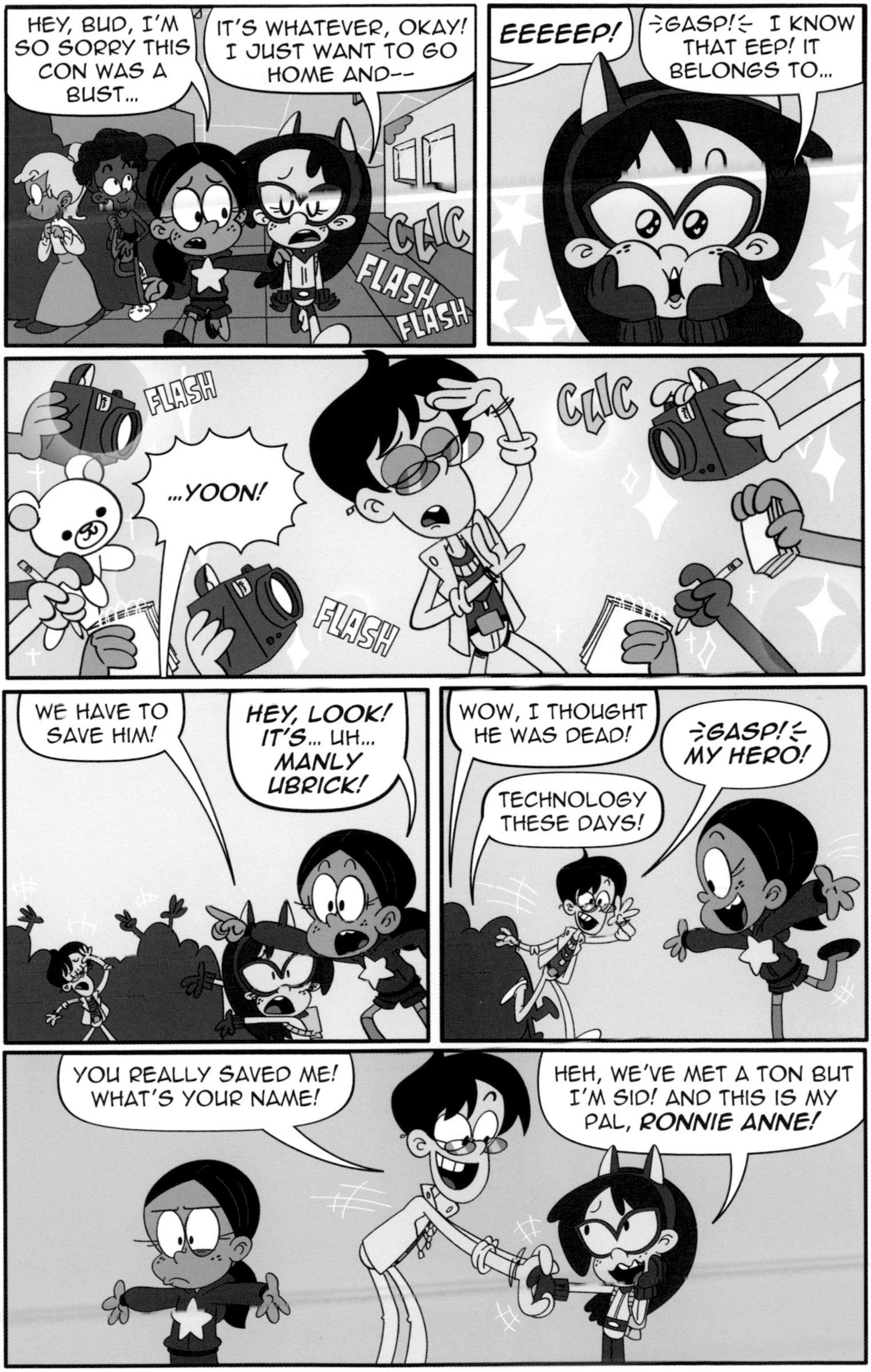
HEY, BUD, I'M SO SORRY THIS CON WAS A BUST...
IT'S WHATEVER, OKAY! I JUST WANT TO GO HOME AND--
CLIC
FLASH
FLASH
EEEEEEP!
GASP! I KNOW THAT EEP! IT BELONGS TO...
FLASH
CLIC
...YOON!
FLASH
WE HAVE TO SAVE HIM!
HEY, LOOK! IT'S... UH... MANLY UBRICK!
WOW, I THOUGHT HE WAS DEAD!
GASP! MY HERO!
TECHNOLOGY THESE DAYS!
YOU REALLY SAVED ME! WHAT'S YOUR NAME!
HEH, WE'VE MET A TON BUT I'M SID! AND THIS IS MY PAL, RONNIE ANNE!

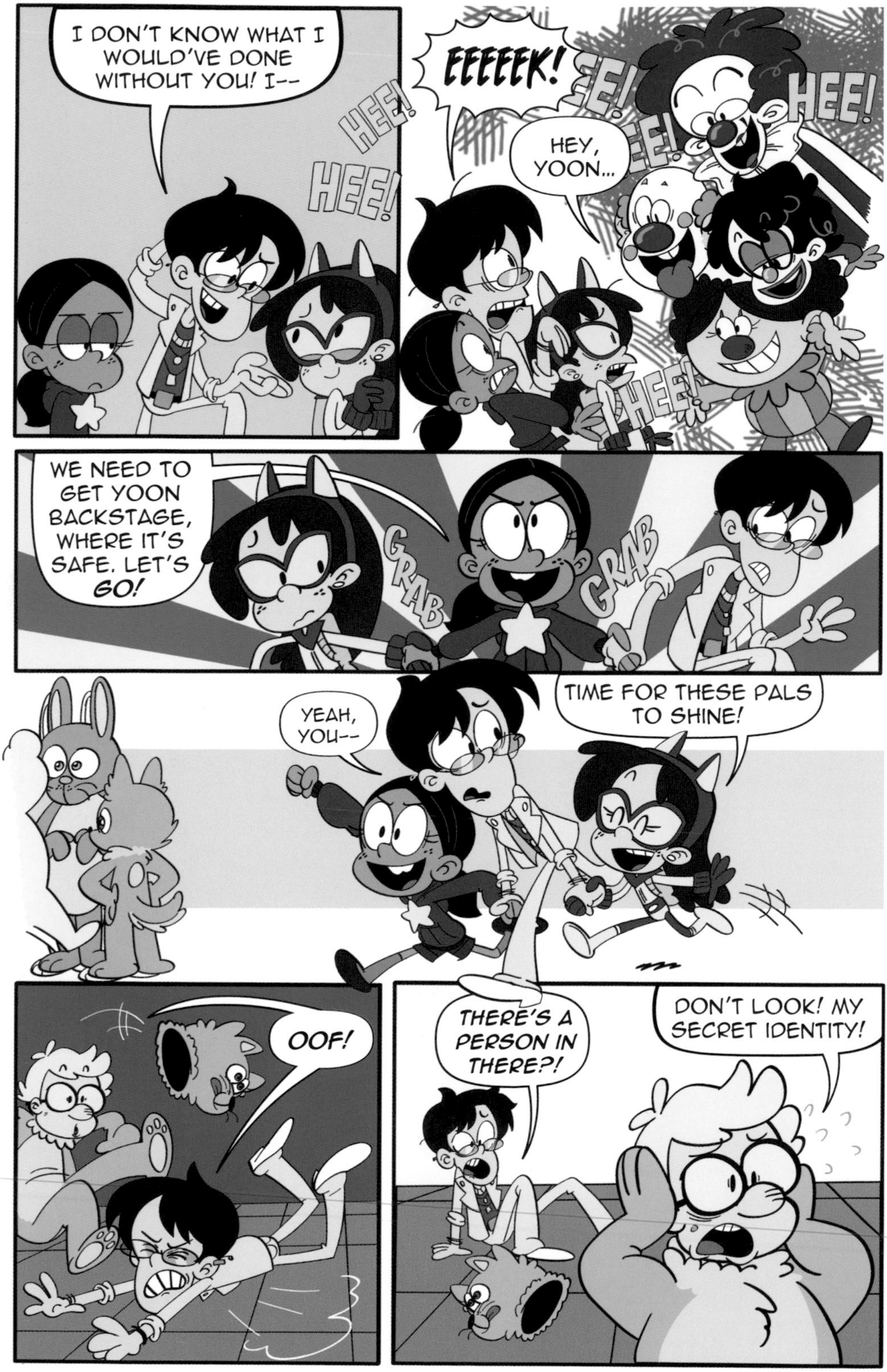
I DON'T KNOW WHAT I WOULD'VE DONE WITHOUT YOU! I--
HEE!
HEE!
EEEEEK!
EE!
HEY, YOON...
EE!
HEE!
HEE!
WE NEED TO GET YOON BACKSTAGE, WHERE IT'S SAFE. LET'S *GO!*
GRAB
GRAB
YEAH, YOU--
TIME FOR THESE PALS TO SHINE!
OOF!
THERE'S A PERSON IN THERE?!
DON'T LOOK! MY SECRET IDENTITY!

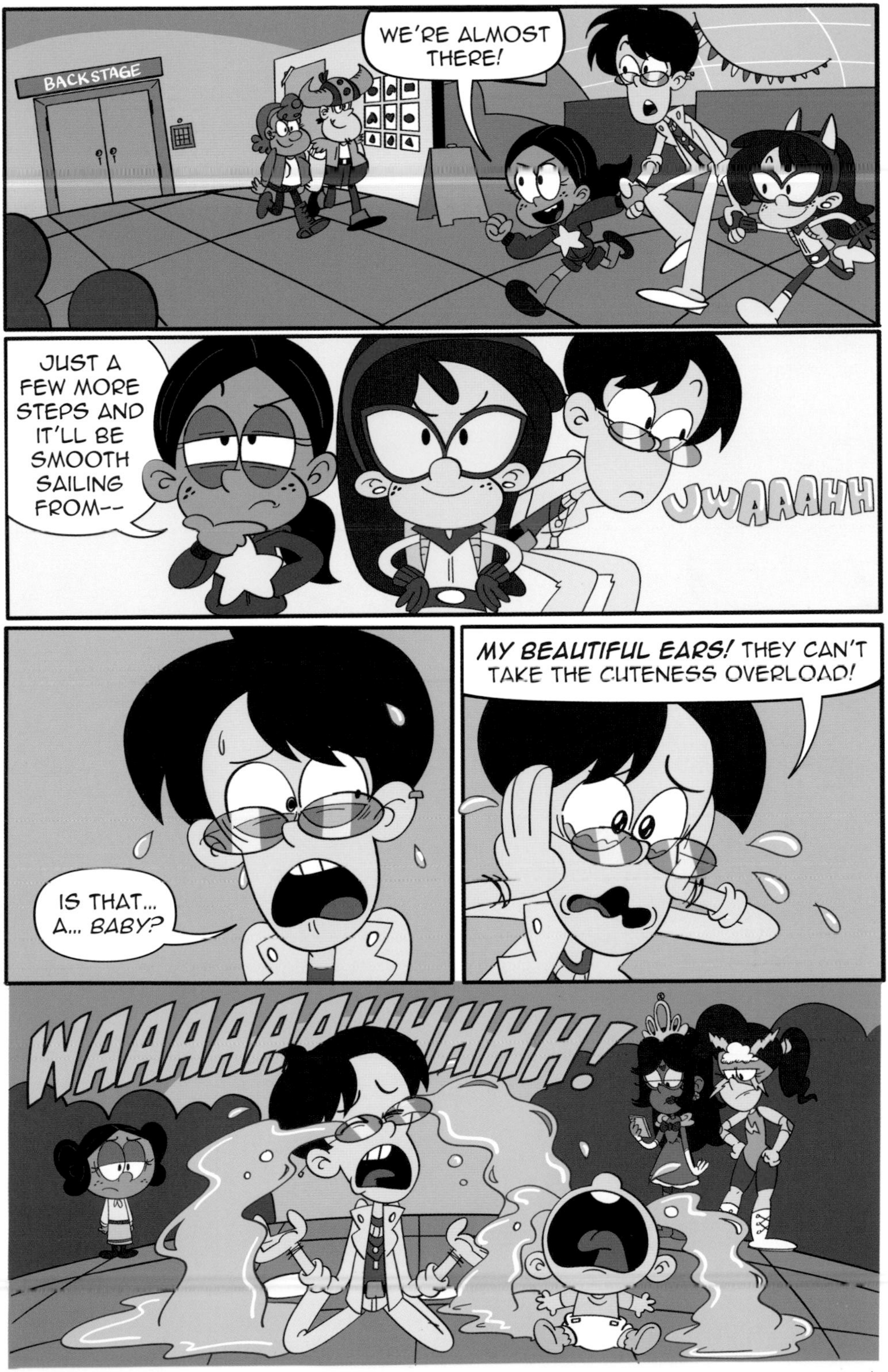
BACKSTAGE
WE'RE ALMOST THERE!
JUST A FEW MORE STEPS AND IT'LL BE SMOOTH SAILING FROM--
UWAAAAHH
IS THAT... A... BABY?
MY BEAUTIFUL EARS! THEY CAN'T TAKE THE CUTENESS OVERLOAD!
WAAAAAAHHHHH!

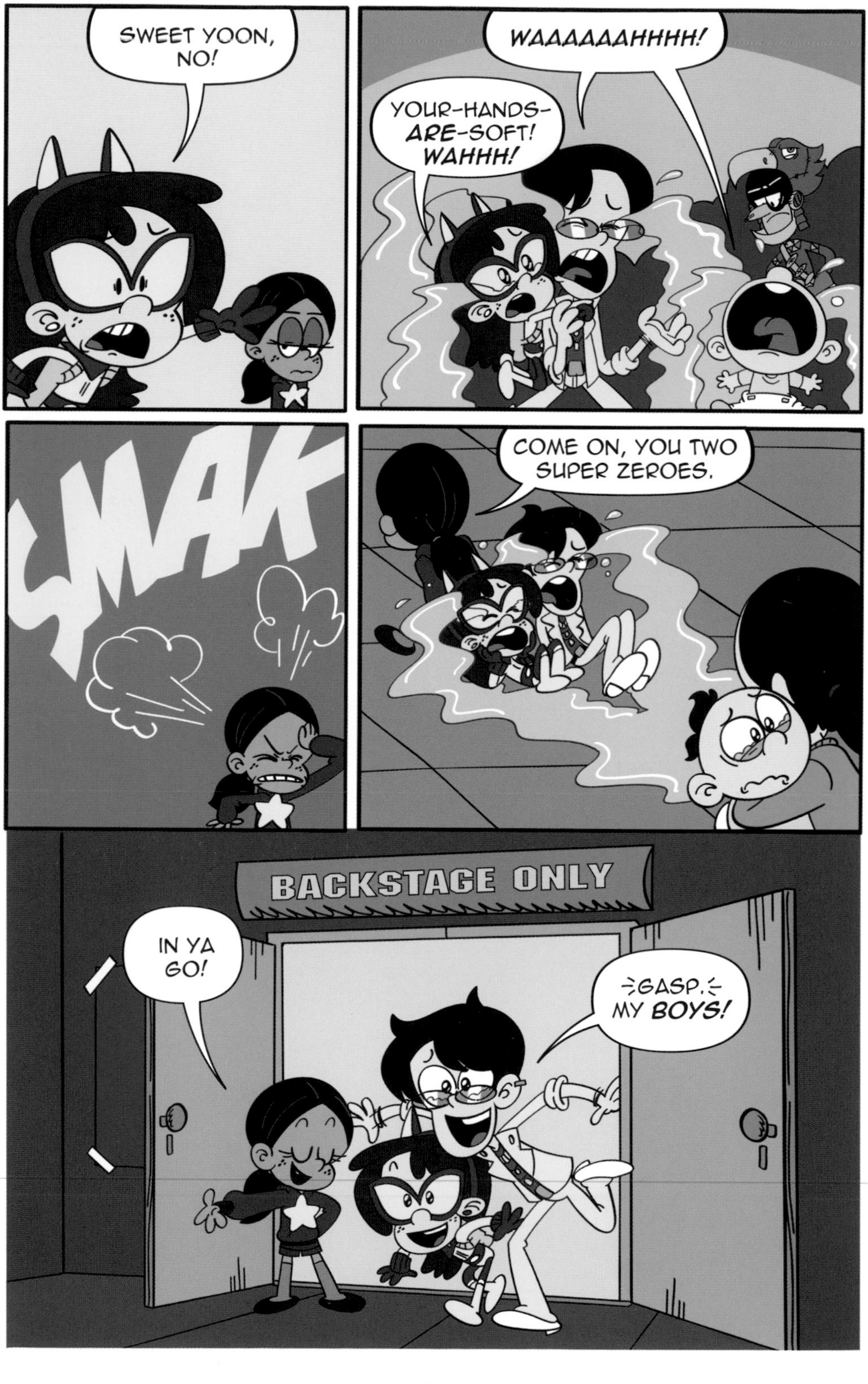
SWEET YOON, NO!
WAAAAAAHHHH!
YOUR-HANDS-ARE-SOFT! WAHHH!
SMAK
COME ON, YOU TWO SUPER ZEROES.
BACKSTAGE ONLY
IN YA GO!
GASP. MY BOYS!

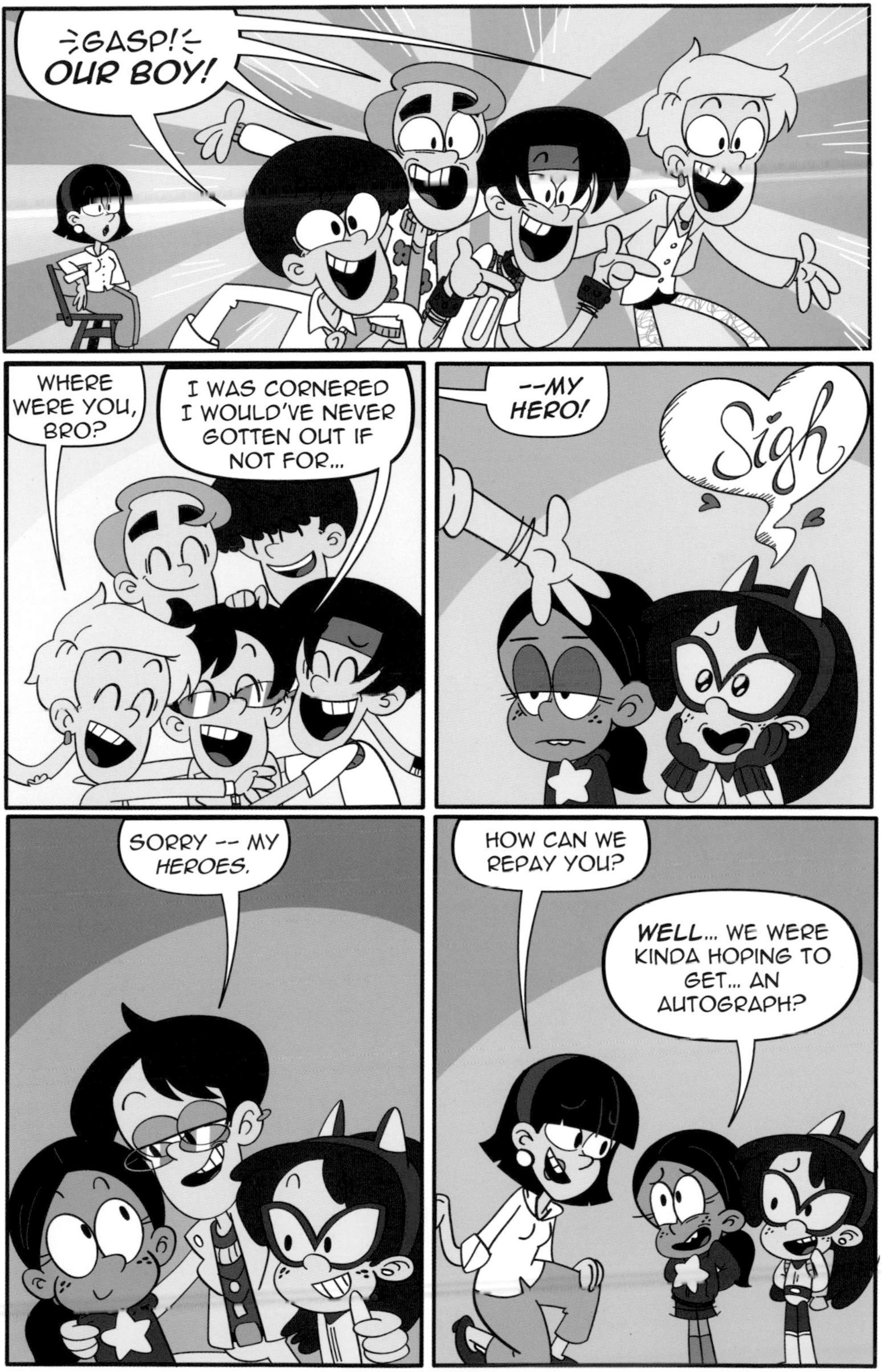
GASP! OUR BOY!
WHERE WERE YOU, BRO?
I WAS CORNERED I WOULD'VE NEVER GOTTEN OUT IF NOT FOR...
--MY HERO!
Sigh
SORRY -- MY HEROES.
HOW CAN WE REPAY YOU?
WELL... WE WERE KINDA HOPING TO GET... AN AUTOGRAPH?

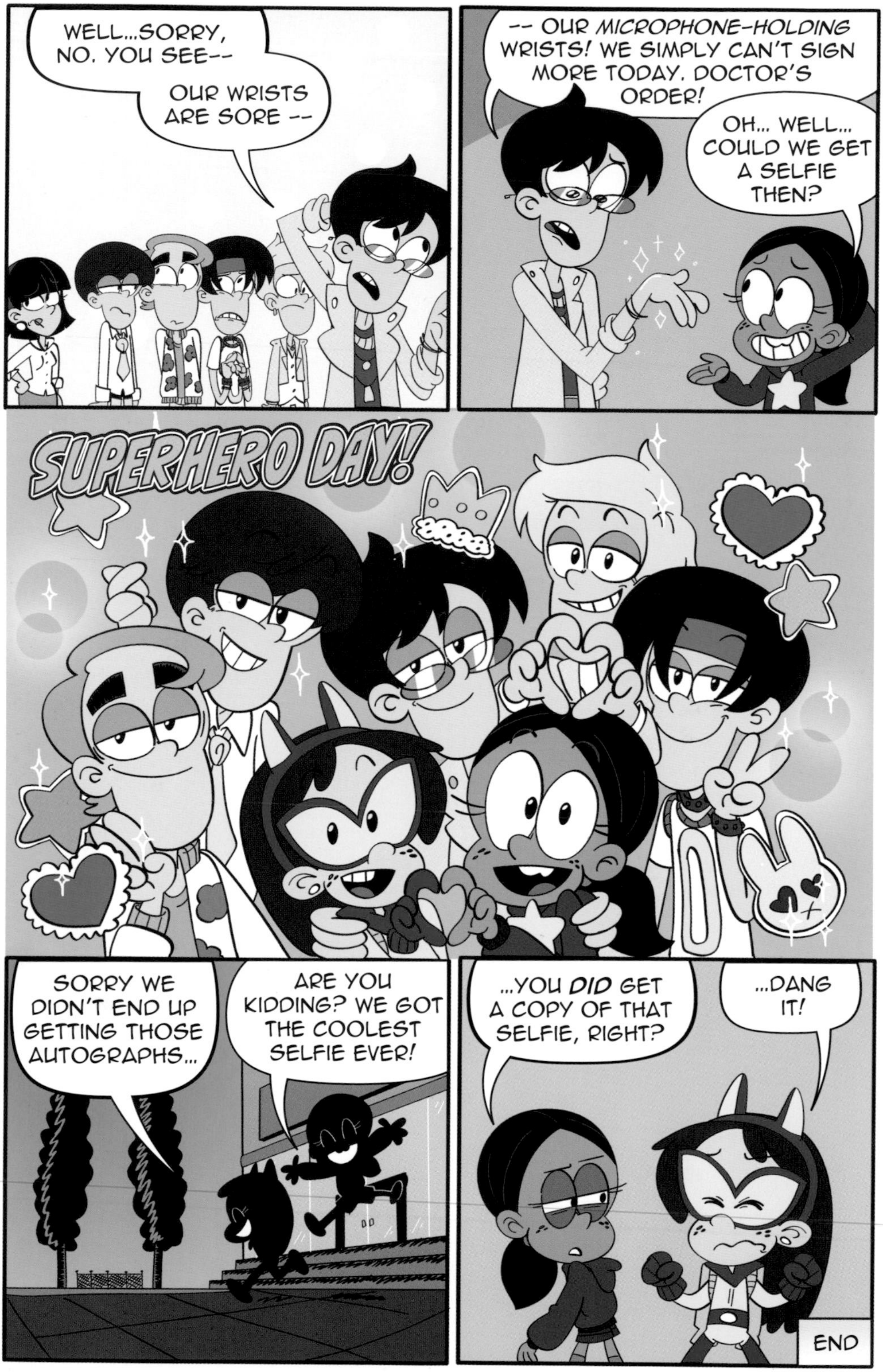
WELL...SORRY, NO. YOU SEE--
OUR WRISTS ARE SORE --
-- OUR *MICROPHONE-HOLDING* WRISTS! WE SIMPLY CAN'T SIGN MORE TODAY. DOCTOR'S ORDER!
OH... WELL... COULD WE GET A SELFIE THEN?
SUPERHERO DAY!
SORRY WE DIDN'T END UP GETTING THOSE AUTOGRAPHS...
ARE YOU KIDDING? WE GOT THE COOLEST SELFIE EVER!
...YOU ***DID*** GET A COPY OF THAT SELFIE, RIGHT?
...DANG *IT!*
END

"SHREDDED BEEF"

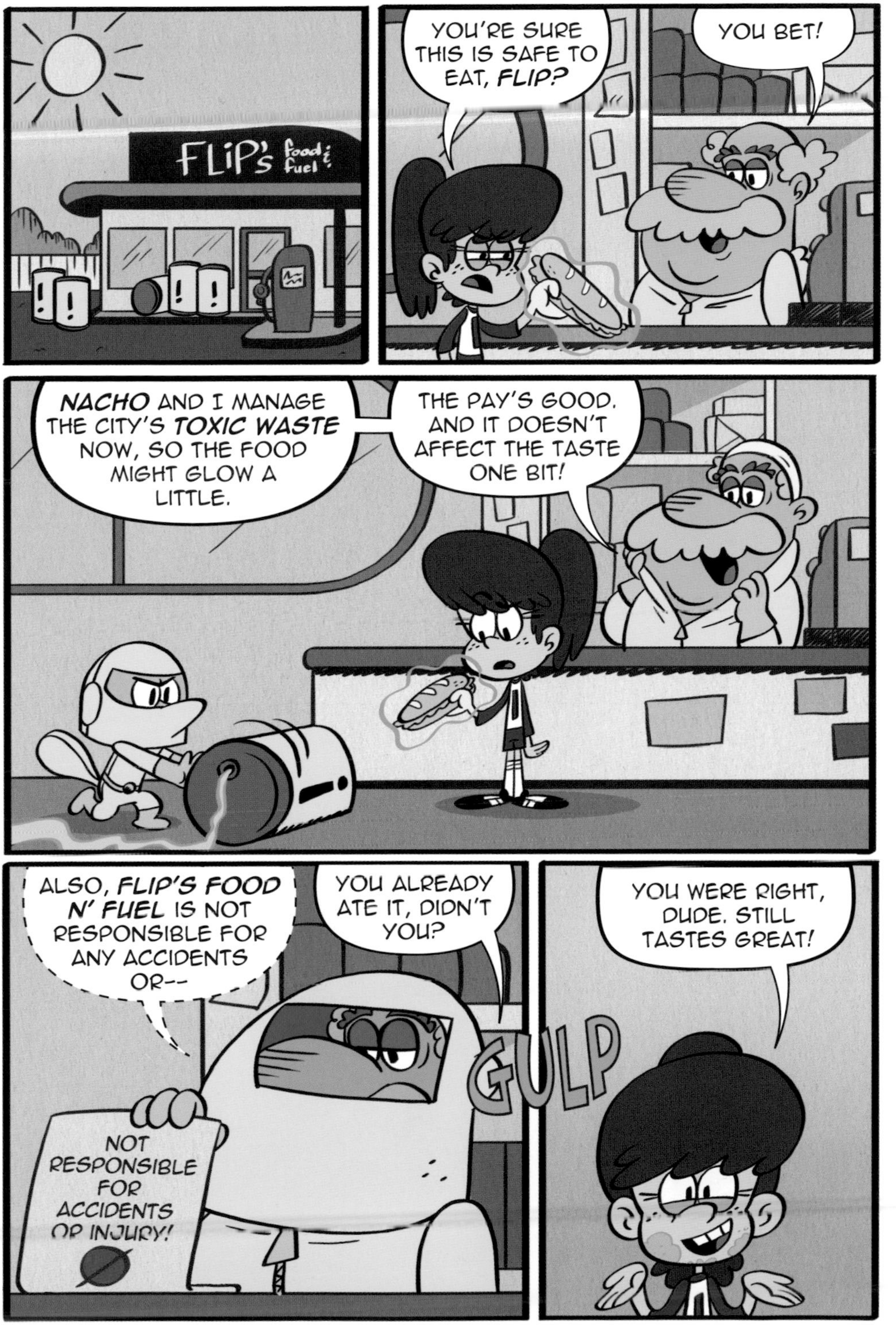
FLIP'S food & fuel
YOU'RE SURE THIS IS SAFE TO EAT, FLIP?
YOU BET!
NACHO AND I MANAGE THE CITY'S TOXIC WASTE NOW, SO THE FOOD MIGHT GLOW A LITTLE.
THE PAY'S GOOD. AND IT DOESN'T AFFECT THE TASTE ONE BIT!
ALSO, FLIP'S FOOD N' FUEL IS NOT RESPONSIBLE FOR ANY ACCIDENTS OR--
YOU ALREADY ATE IT, DIDN'T YOU?
NOT RESPONSIBLE FOR ACCIDENTS OR INJURY!
GULP
YOU WERE RIGHT, DUDE. STILL TASTES GREAT!

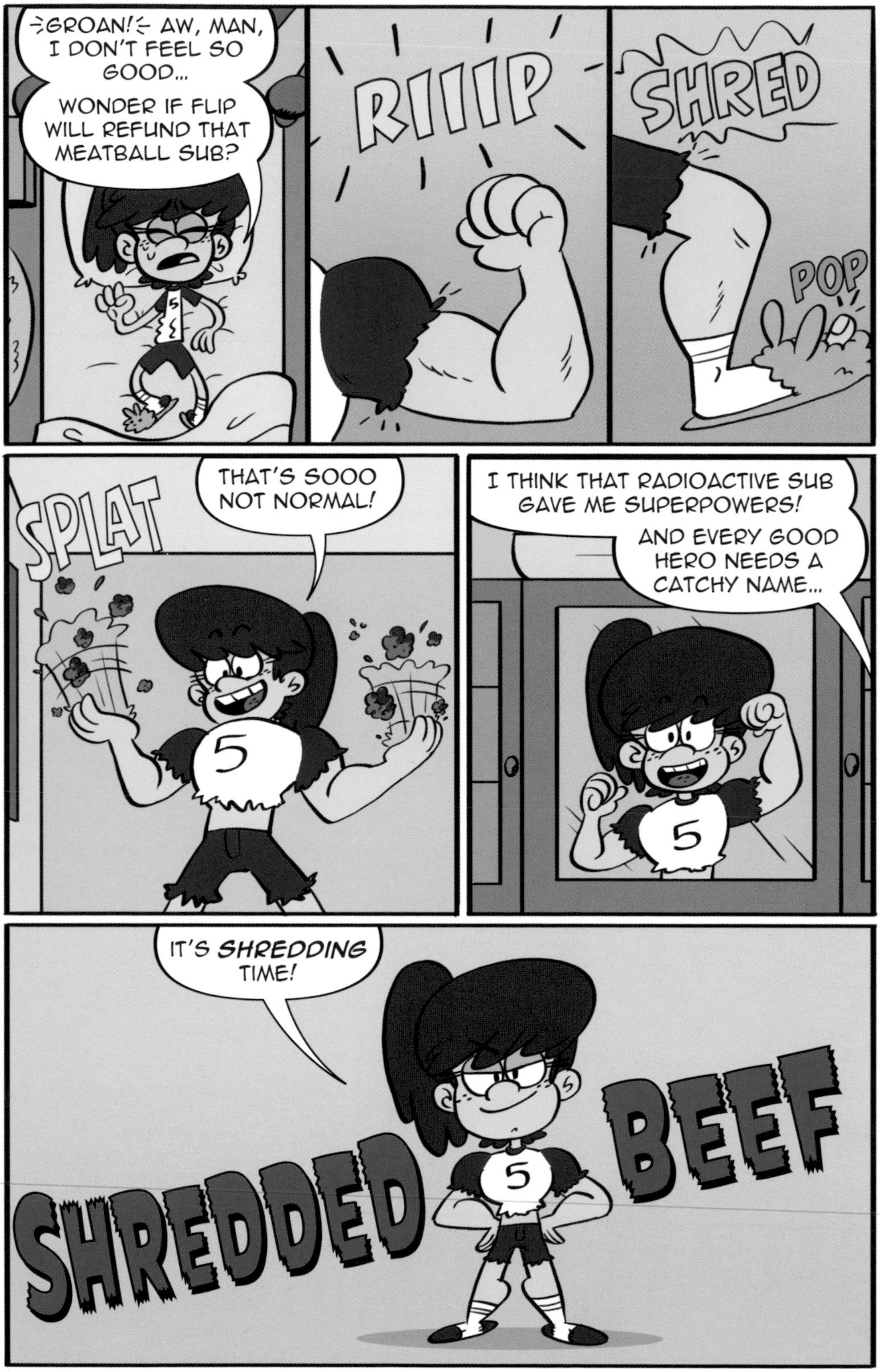
GROAN! AW, MAN, I DON'T FEEL SO GOOD...
WONDER IF FLIP WILL REFUND THAT MEATBALL SUB?
RIIIP
SHRED
POP
SPLAT
THAT'S SOOO NOT NORMAL!
I THINK THAT RADIOACTIVE SUB GAVE ME SUPERPOWERS!
AND EVERY GOOD HERO NEEDS A CATCHY NAME...
IT'S SHREDDING TIME!
SHREDDED BEEF

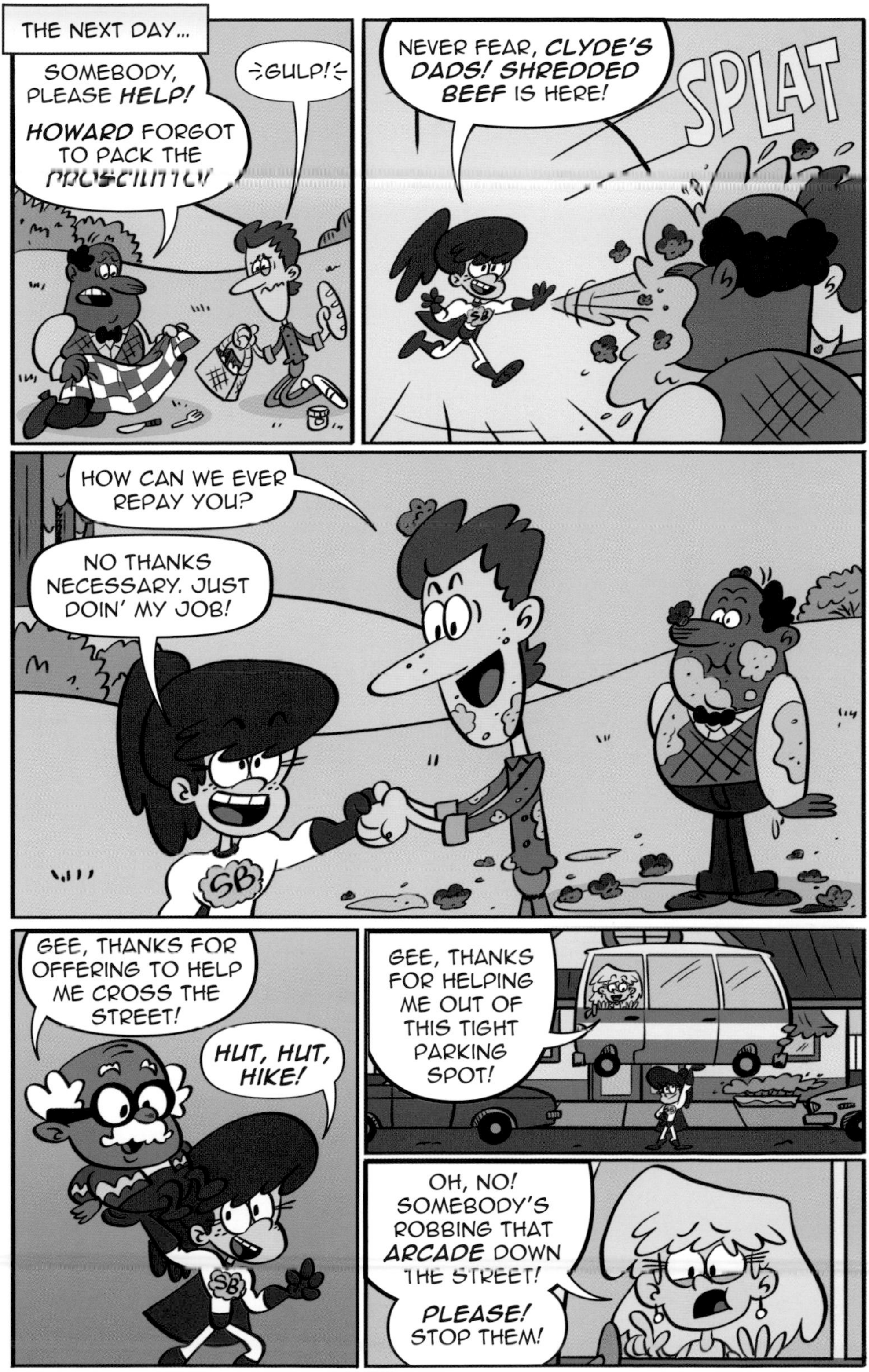
THE NEXT DAY...
SOMEBODY, PLEASE HELP!
HOWARD FORGOT TO PACK THE
GULP!
NEVER FEAR, CLYDE'S DADS! SHREDDED BEEF IS HERE!
SPLAT
HOW CAN WE EVER REPAY YOU?
NO THANKS NECESSARY. JUST DOIN' MY JOB!
GEE, THANKS FOR OFFERING TO HELP ME CROSS THE STREET!
HUT, HUT, HIKE!
GEE, THANKS FOR HELPING ME OUT OF THIS TIGHT PARKING SPOT!
OH, NO! SOMEBODY'S ROBBING THAT ARCADE DOWN THE STREET!
PLEASE! STOP THEM!

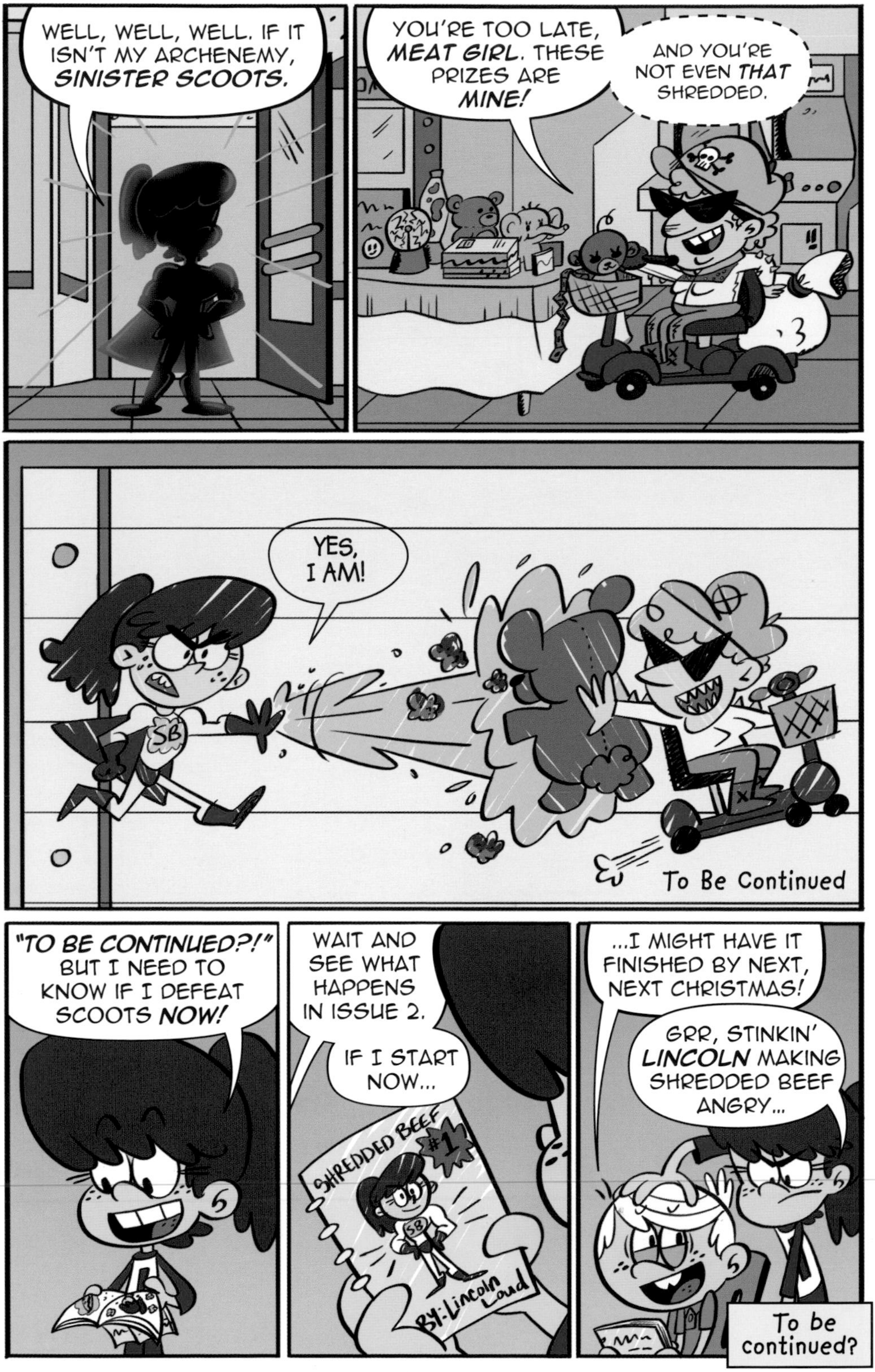

WELL, WELL, WELL. IF IT ISN'T MY ARCHENEMY, SINISTER SCOOTS.
YOU'RE TOO LATE, MEAT GIRL. THESE PRIZES ARE MINE!
AND YOU'RE NOT EVEN THAT SHREDDED.
YES, I AM!
To Be Continued
"TO BE CONTINUED?!" BUT I NEED TO KNOW IF I DEFEAT SCOOTS NOW!
WAIT AND SEE WHAT HAPPENS IN ISSUE 2.
IF I START NOW...
SHREDDED BEEF #1
SB
BY: Lincoln Loud
...I MIGHT HAVE IT FINISHED BY NEXT, NEXT CHRISTMAS!
GRR, STINKIN' LINCOLN MAKING SHREDDED BEEF ANGRY...
To be continued?

"THE CROWNED CAPER"

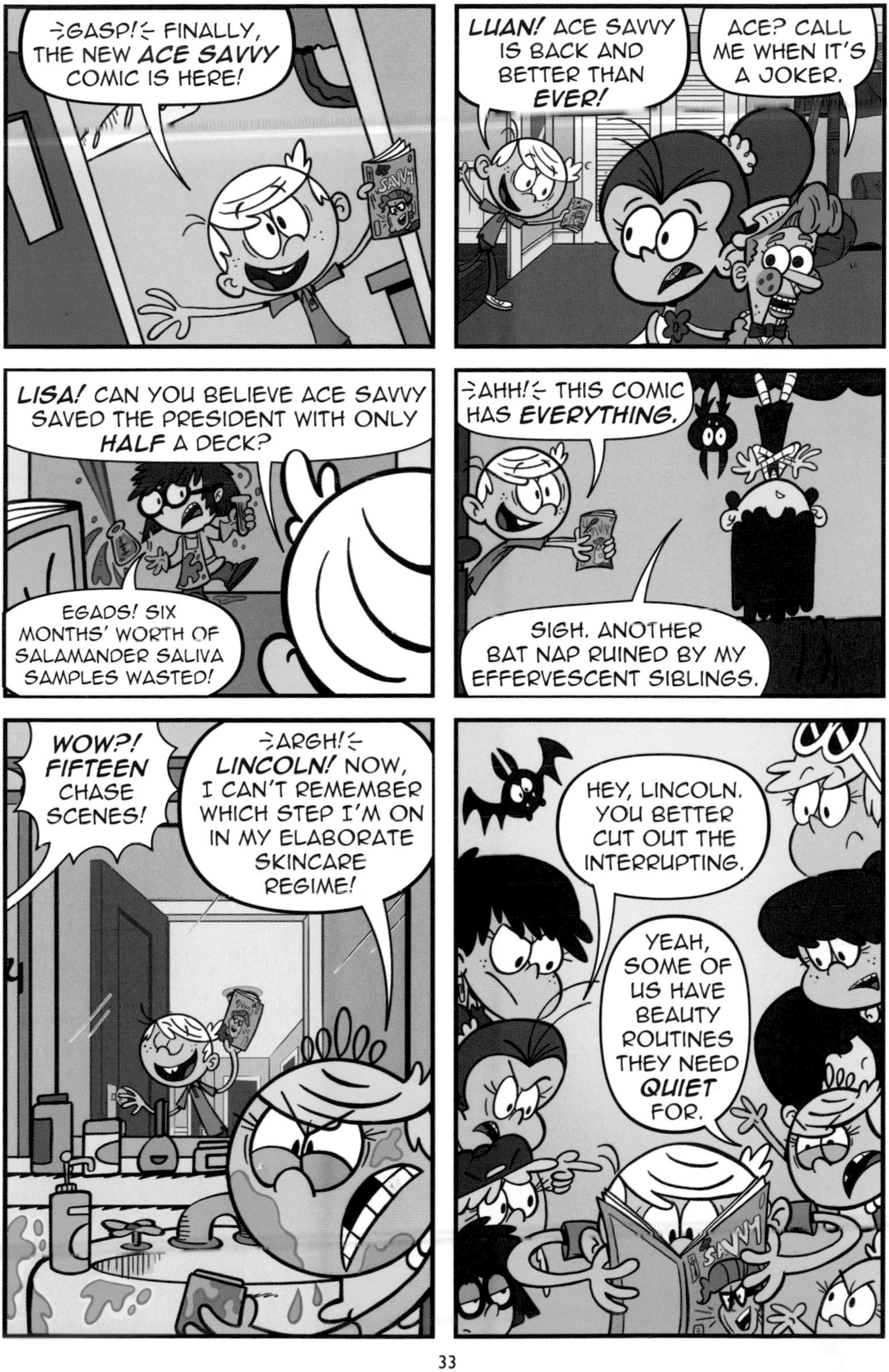

GASP! FINALLY, THE NEW ACE SAVVY COMIC IS HERE!
LUAN! ACE SAVVY IS BACK AND BETTER THAN EVER!
ACE? CALL ME WHEN IT'S A JOKER.
LISA! CAN YOU BELIEVE ACE SAVVY SAVED THE PRESIDENT WITH ONLY HALF A DECK?
EGADS! SIX MONTHS' WORTH OF SALAMANDER SALIVA SAMPLES WASTED!
AHH! THIS COMIC HAS EVERYTHING.
SIGH. ANOTHER BAT NAP RUINED BY MY EFFERVESCENT SIBLINGS.
WOW?! FIFTEEN CHASE SCENES!
ARGH! LINCOLN! NOW, I CAN'T REMEMBER WHICH STEP I'M ON IN MY ELABORATE SKINCARE REGIME!
HEY, LINCOLN. YOU BETTER CUT OUT THE INTERRUPTING.
YEAH, SOME OF US HAVE BEAUTY ROUTINES THEY NEED QUIET FOR.

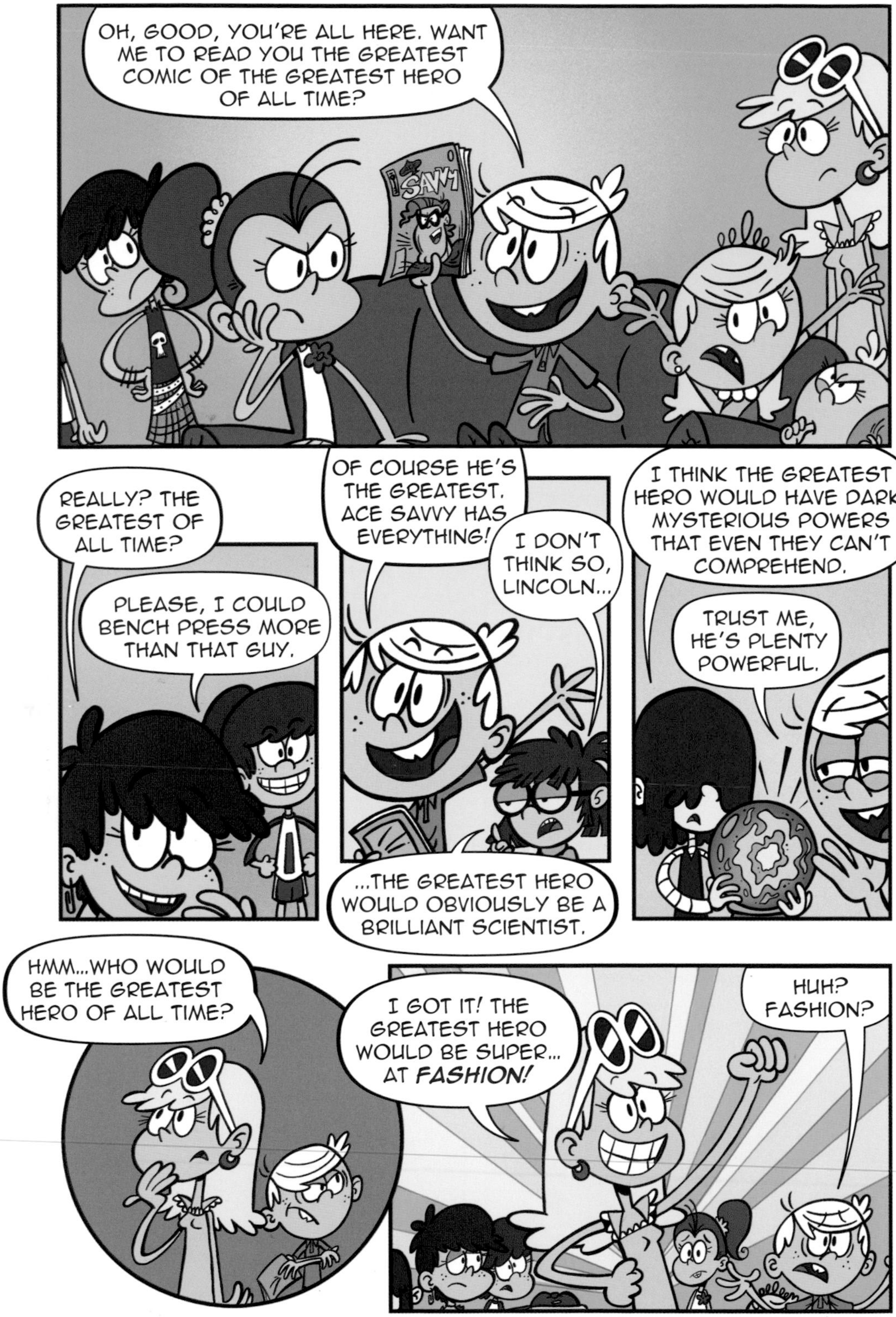
OH, GOOD, YOU'RE ALL HERE. WANT ME TO READ YOU THE GREATEST COMIC OF THE GREATEST HERO OF ALL TIME?
REALLY? THE GREATEST OF ALL TIME?
PLEASE, I COULD BENCH PRESS MORE THAN THAT GUY.
OF COURSE HE'S THE GREATEST. ACE SAVVY HAS EVERYTHING!
I DON'T THINK SO, LINCOLN...
...THE GREATEST HERO WOULD OBVIOUSLY BE A BRILLIANT SCIENTIST.
I THINK THE GREATEST HERO WOULD HAVE DARK, MYSTERIOUS POWERS THAT EVEN THEY CAN'T COMPREHEND.
TRUST ME, HE'S PLENTY POWERFUL.
HMM...WHO WOULD BE THE GREATEST HERO OF ALL TIME?
I GOT IT! THE GREATEST HERO WOULD BE SUPER... AT FASHION!
HUH? FASHION?

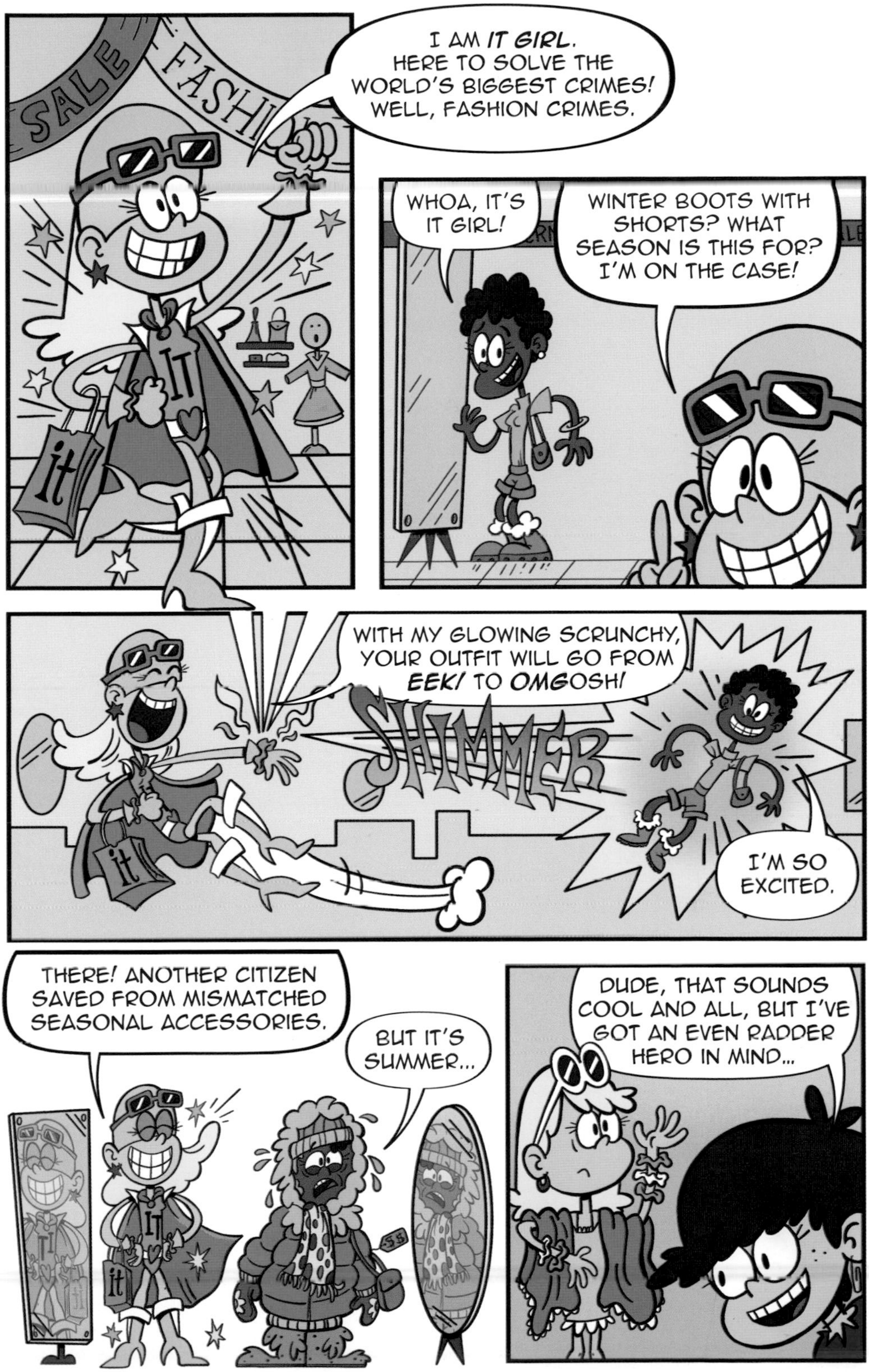
SALE
FASHI
I AM IT GIRL. HERE TO SOLVE THE WORLD'S BIGGEST CRIMES! WELL, FASHION CRIMES.
WHOA, IT'S IT GIRL!
WINTER BOOTS WITH SHORTS? WHAT SEASON IS THIS FOR? I'M ON THE CASE!
WITH MY GLOWING SCRUNCHY, YOUR OUTFIT WILL GO FROM EEK! TO OMGOSH!
SHIMMER
I'M SO EXCITED.
THERE! ANOTHER CITIZEN SAVED FROM MISMATCHED SEASONAL ACCESSORIES.
BUT IT'S SUMMER...
DUDE, THAT SOUNDS COOL AND ALL, BUT I'VE GOT AN EVEN RADDER HERO IN MIND...

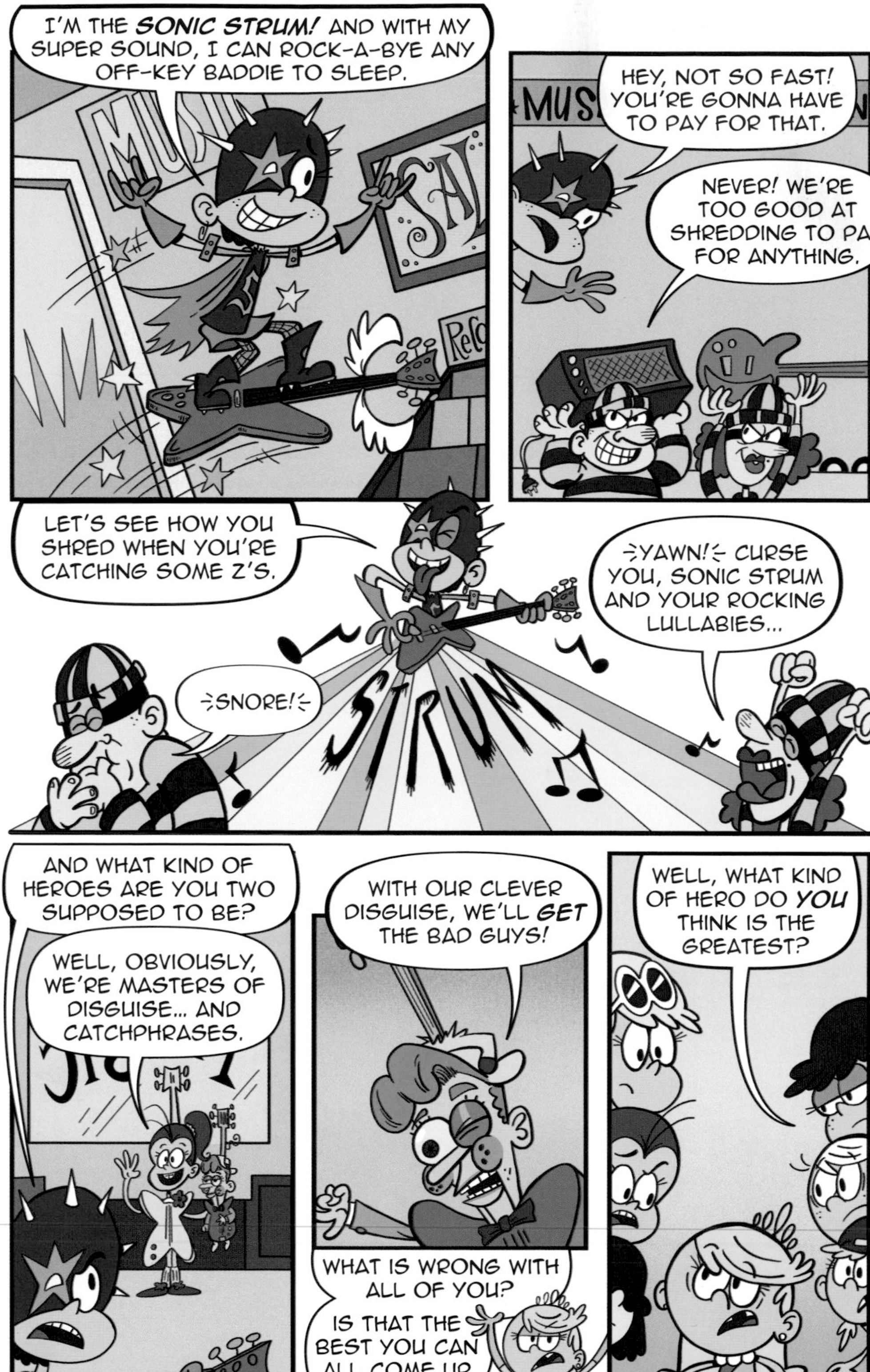

I'M THE ***SONIC STRUM!*** AND WITH MY SUPER SOUND, I CAN ROCK-A-BYE ANY OFF-KEY BADDIE TO SLEEP.
HEY, NOT SO FAST! YOU'RE GONNA HAVE TO PAY FOR THAT.
NEVER! WE'RE TOO GOOD AT SHREDDING TO PAY FOR ANYTHING.
LET'S SEE HOW YOU SHRED WHEN YOU'RE CATCHING SOME Z'S.
YAWN! CURSE YOU, SONIC STRUM AND YOUR ROCKING LULLABIES...
SNORE!
STRUM
AND WHAT KIND OF HEROES ARE YOU TWO SUPPOSED TO BE?
WELL, OBVIOUSLY, WE'RE MASTERS OF DISGUISE... AND CATCHPHRASES.
WITH OUR CLEVER DISGUISE, WE'LL ***GET*** THE BAD GUYS!
WHAT IS WRONG WITH ALL OF YOU?
IS THAT THE BEST YOU CAN ALL COME UP WITH?
WELL, WHAT KIND OF HERO DO ***YOU*** THINK IS THE GREATEST?

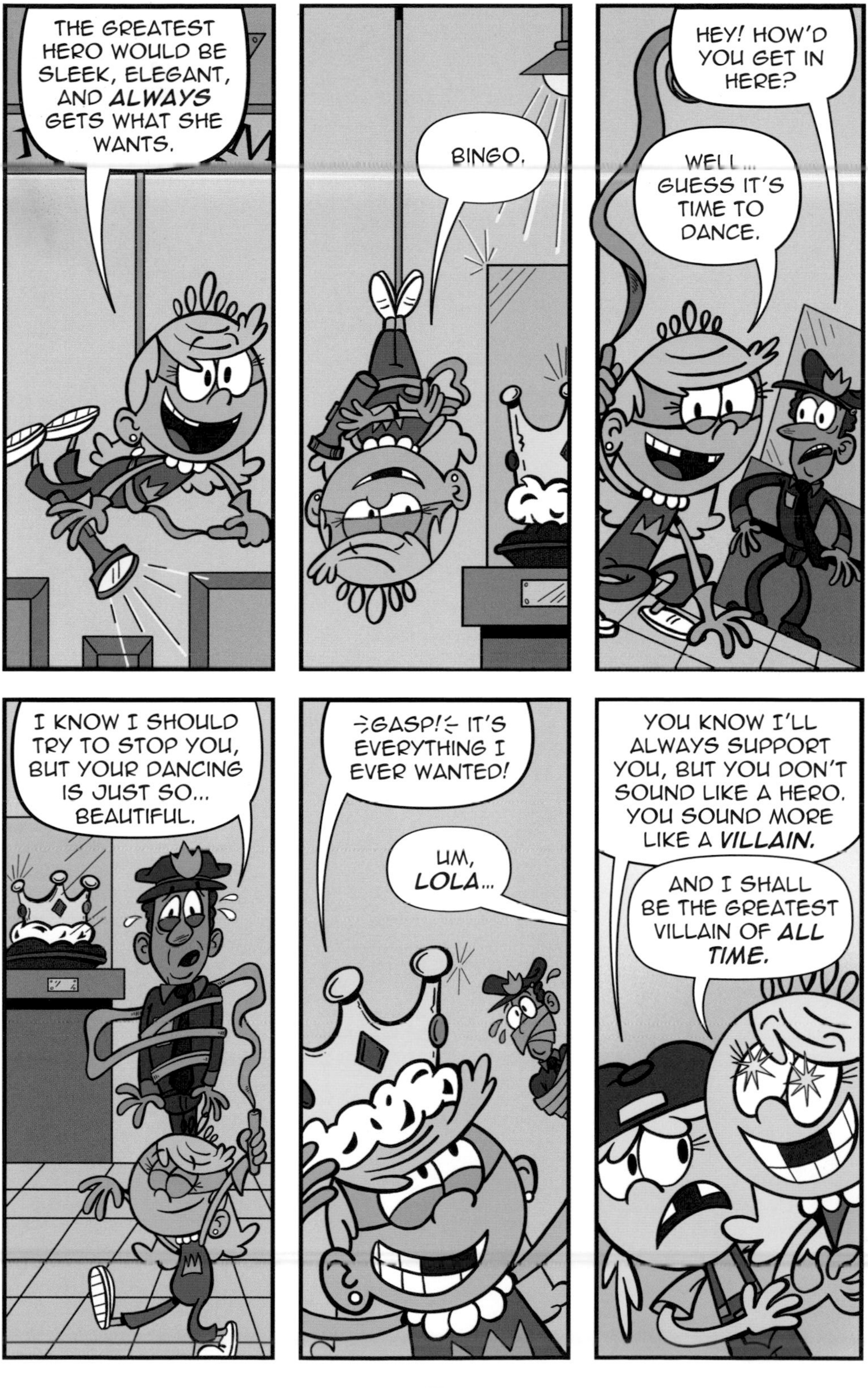
THE GREATEST HERO WOULD BE SLEEK, ELEGANT, AND ALWAYS GETS WHAT SHE WANTS.
BINGO.
HEY! HOW'D YOU GET IN HERE?
WELL... GUESS IT'S TIME TO DANCE.
I KNOW I SHOULD TRY TO STOP YOU, BUT YOUR DANCING IS JUST SO... BEAUTIFUL.
GASP! IT'S EVERYTHING I EVER WANTED!
UM, LOLA...
YOU KNOW I'LL ALWAYS SUPPORT YOU, BUT YOU DON'T SOUND LIKE A HERO. YOU SOUND MORE LIKE A VILLAIN.
AND I SHALL BE THE GREATEST VILLAIN OF ALL TIME.

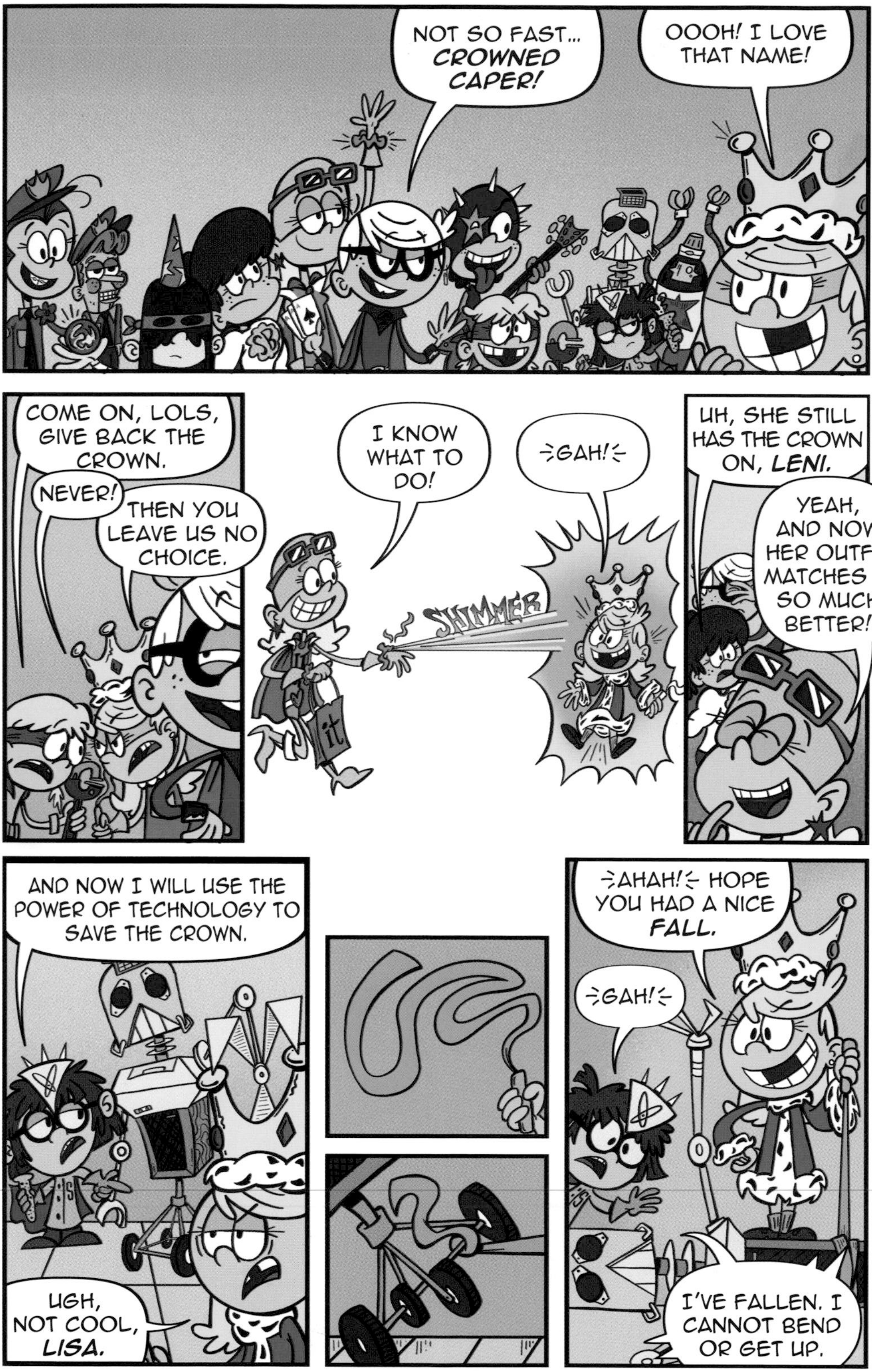
NOT SO FAST... CROWNED CAPER!
OOOH! I LOVE THAT NAME!
COME ON, LOLS, GIVE BACK THE CROWN.
NEVER!
THEN YOU LEAVE US NO CHOICE.
I KNOW WHAT TO DO!
SHIMMER
GAH!
UH, SHE STILL HAS THE CROWN ON, LENI.
YEAH, AND NOW HER OUTFIT MATCHES IT SO MUCH BETTER!
AND NOW I WILL USE THE POWER OF TECHNOLOGY TO SAVE THE CROWN.
UGH, NOT COOL, LISA.
AHAH! HOPE YOU HAD A NICE FALL.
GAH!
I'VE FALLEN. I CANNOT BEND OR GET UP.

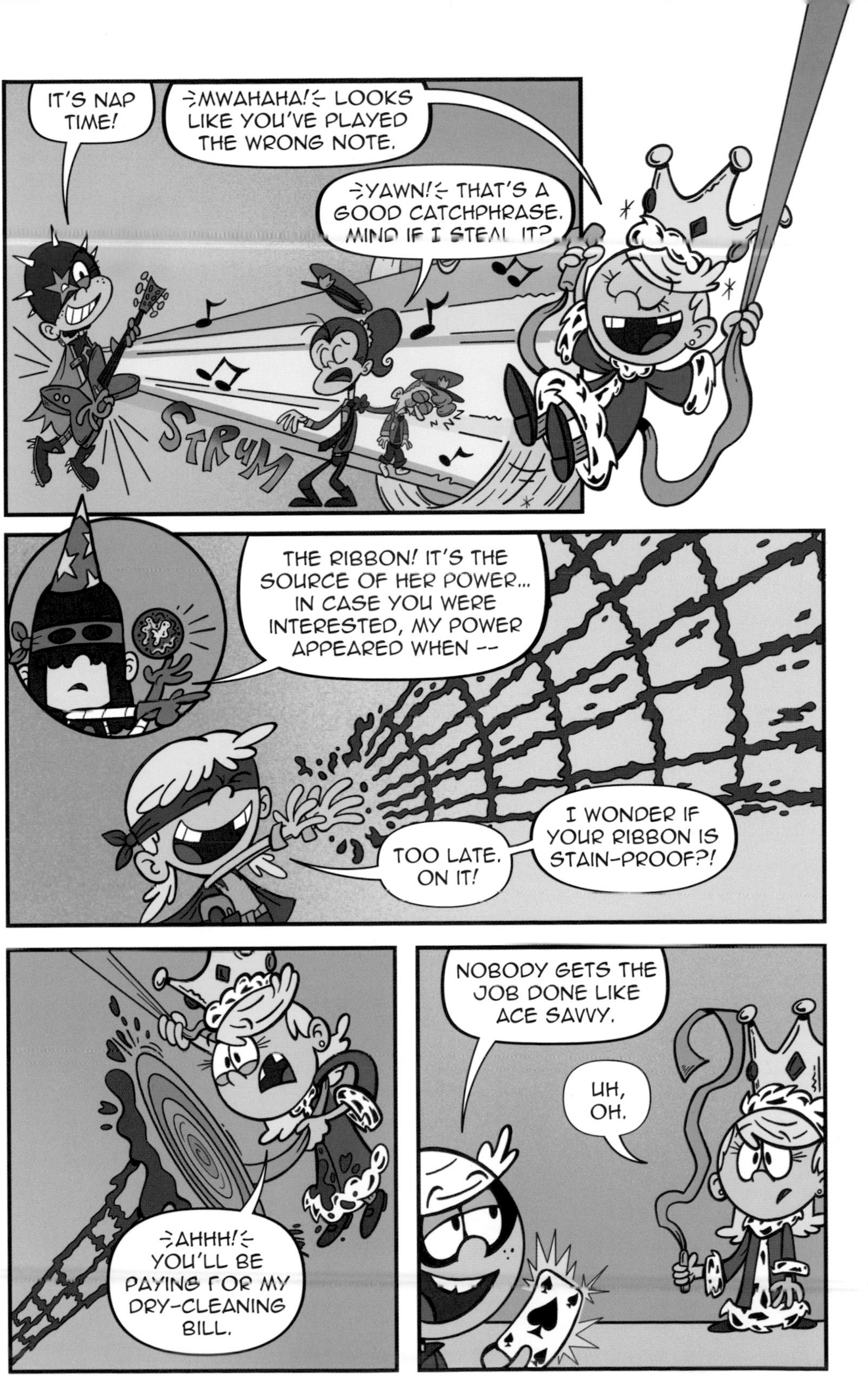
IT'S NAP TIME!
-MWAHAHA!- LOOKS LIKE YOU'VE PLAYED THE WRONG NOTE.
-YAWN!- THAT'S A GOOD CATCHPHRASE. MIND IF I STEAL IT?
STRUM
THE RIBBON! IT'S THE SOURCE OF HER POWER... IN CASE YOU WERE INTERESTED, MY POWER APPEARED WHEN --
I WONDER IF YOUR RIBBON IS STAIN-PROOF?!
TOO LATE. ON IT!
-AHHH!- YOU'LL BE PAYING FOR MY DRY-CLEANING BILL.
NOBODY GETS THE JOB DONE LIKE ACE SAVVY.
UH, OH.

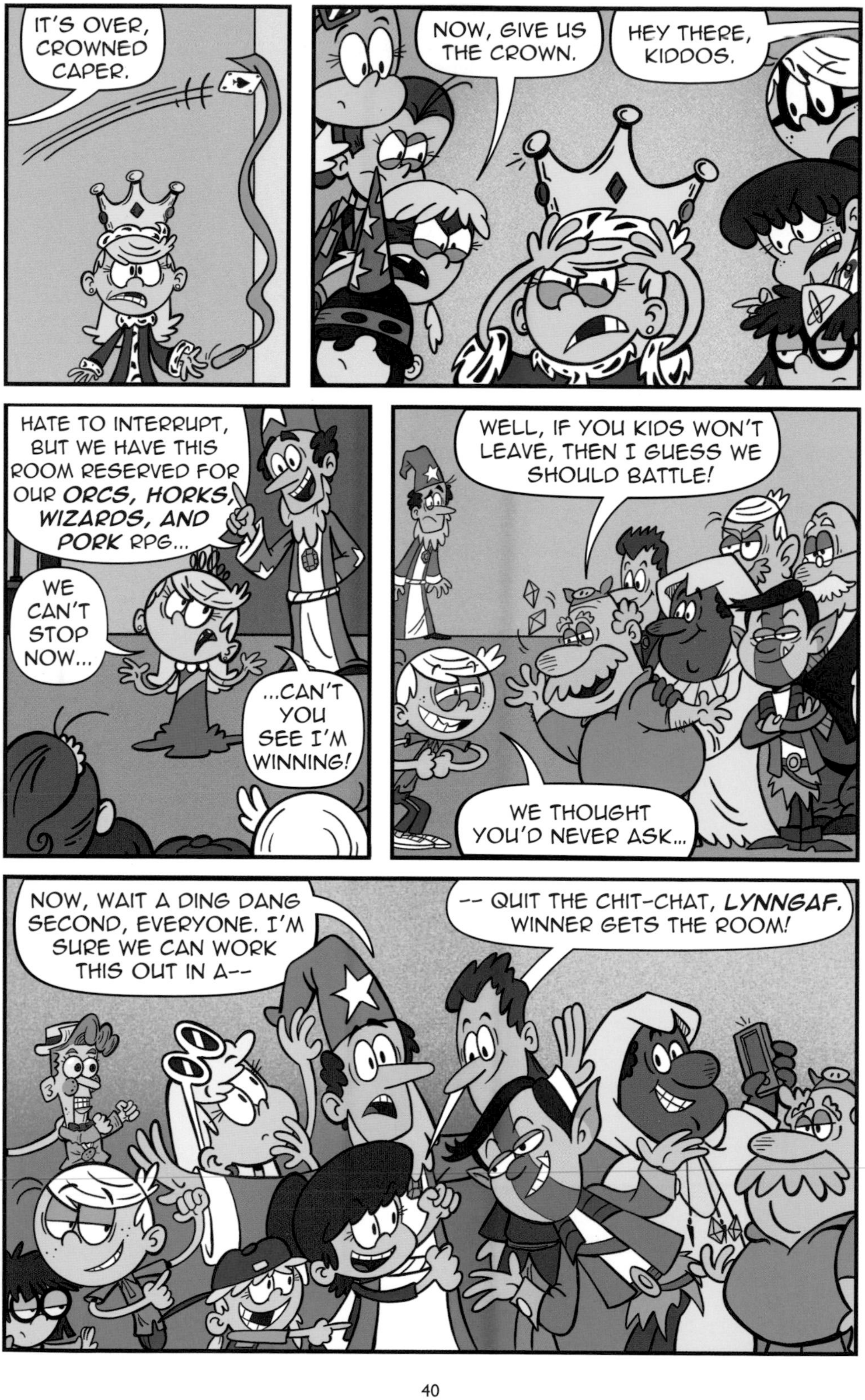
IT'S OVER, CROWNED CAPER.
NOW, GIVE US THE CROWN.
HEY THERE, KIDDOS.
HATE TO INTERRUPT, BUT WE HAVE THIS ROOM RESERVED FOR OUR ORCS, HORKS, WIZARDS, AND PORK RPG...
WE CAN'T STOP NOW...
...CAN'T YOU SEE I'M WINNING!
WELL, IF YOU KIDS WON'T LEAVE, THEN I GUESS WE SHOULD BATTLE!
WE THOUGHT YOU'D NEVER ASK...
NOW, WAIT A DING DANG SECOND, EVERYONE. I'M SURE WE CAN WORK THIS OUT IN A--
-- QUIT THE CHIT-CHAT, LYNNGAF. WINNER GETS THE ROOM!

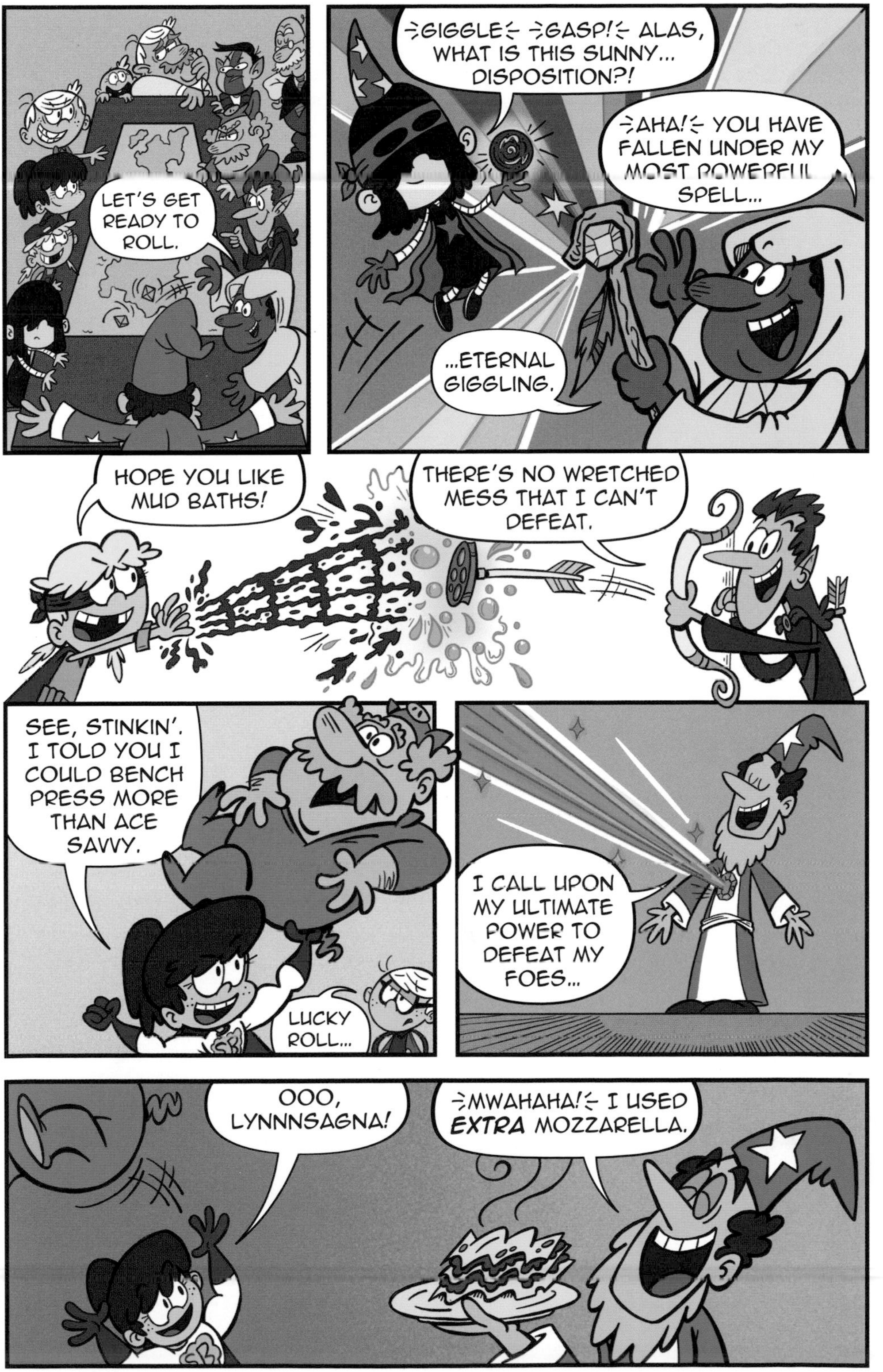
LET'S GET READY TO ROLL.
≑GIGGLE≑ ≑GASP!≑ ALAS, WHAT IS THIS SUNNY... DISPOSITION?!
≑AHA!≑ YOU HAVE FALLEN UNDER MY MOST POWERFUL SPELL...
...ETERNAL GIGGLING.
HOPE YOU LIKE MUD BATHS!
THERE'S NO WRETCHED MESS THAT I CAN'T DEFEAT.
SEE, STINKIN'. I TOLD YOU I COULD BENCH PRESS MORE THAN ACE SAVVY.
LUCKY ROLL...
I CALL UPON MY ULTIMATE POWER TO DEFEAT MY FOES...
OOO, LYNNNSAGNA!
≑MWAHAHA!≑ I USED *EXTRA* MOZZARELLA.

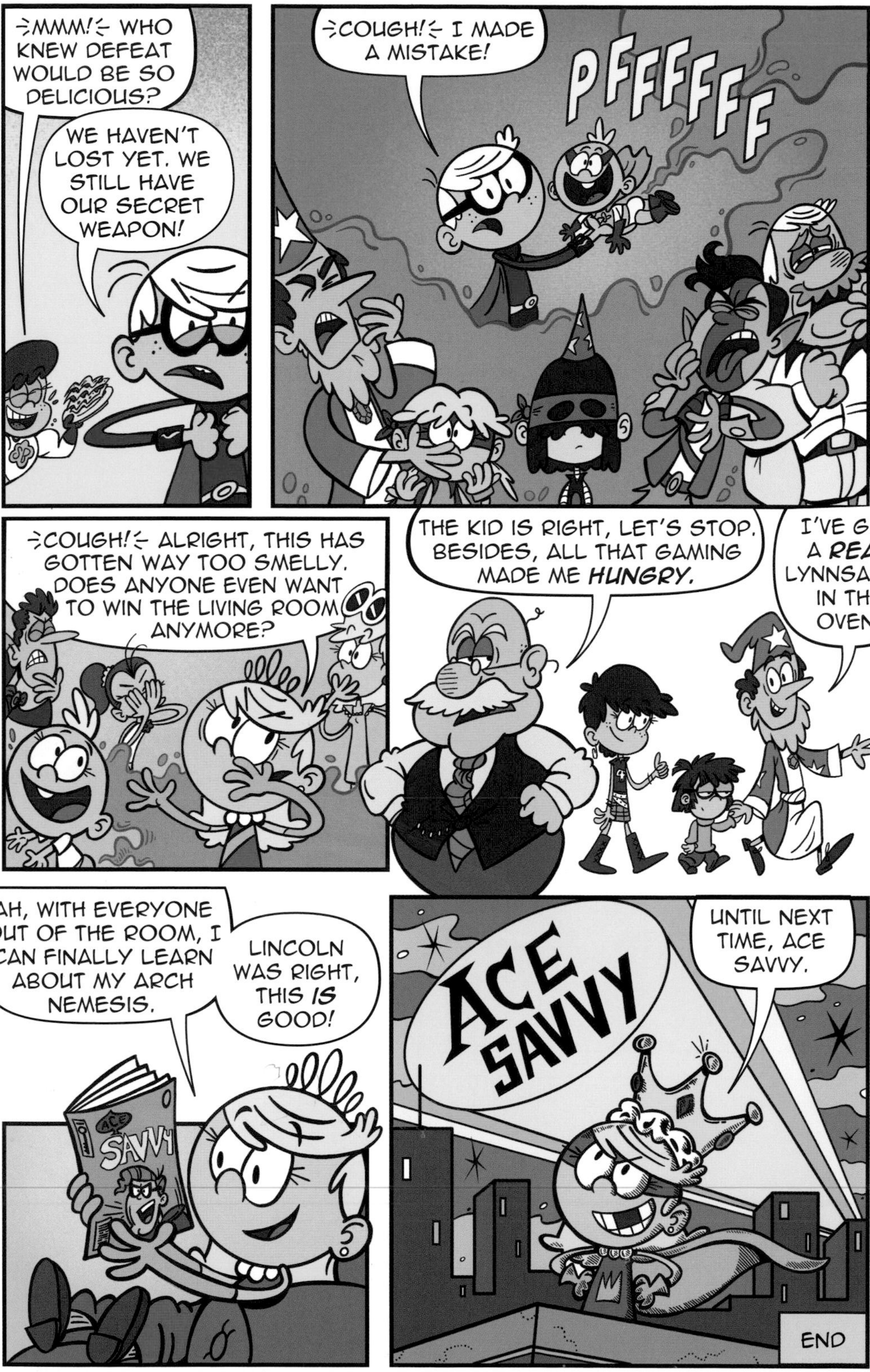

-MMM!- WHO KNEW DEFEAT WOULD BE SO DELICIOUS?
WE HAVEN'T LOST YET. WE STILL HAVE OUR SECRET WEAPON!
-COUGH!- I MADE A MISTAKE!
PFFFFFF
-COUGH!- ALRIGHT, THIS HAS GOTTEN WAY TOO SMELLY. DOES ANYONE EVEN WANT TO WIN THE LIVING ROOM ANYMORE?
THE KID IS RIGHT, LET'S STOP. BESIDES, ALL THAT GAMING MADE ME *HUNGRY*.
I'VE GOT A *REAL* LYNNSAGNA IN THE OVEN!
AH, WITH EVERYONE OUT OF THE ROOM, I CAN FINALLY LEARN ABOUT MY ARCH NEMESIS.
LINCOLN WAS RIGHT, THIS *IS* GOOD!
ACE SAVVY
ACE SAVVY
UNTIL NEXT TIME, ACE SAVVY.
END

"SCENE PARTNER"

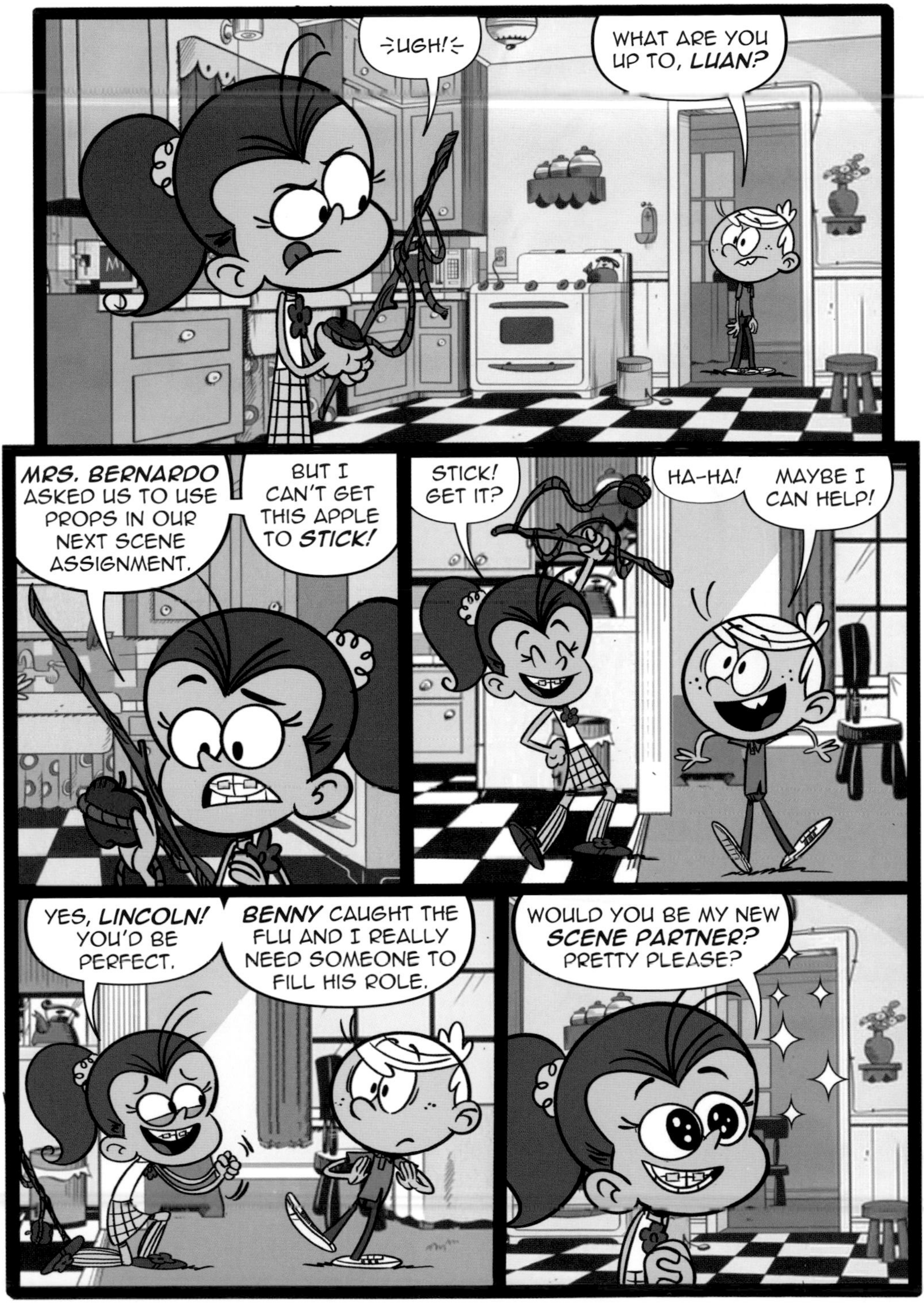

UGH!
WHAT ARE YOU UP TO, LUAN?
MRS. BERNARDO ASKED US TO USE PROPS IN OUR NEXT SCENE ASSIGNMENT.
BUT I CAN'T GET THIS APPLE TO STICK!
STICK! GET IT?
HA-HA!
MAYBE I CAN HELP!
YES, LINCOLN! YOU'D BE PERFECT.
BENNY CAUGHT THE FLU AND I REALLY NEED SOMEONE TO FILL HIS ROLE.
WOULD YOU BE MY NEW SCENE PARTNER? PRETTY PLEASE?

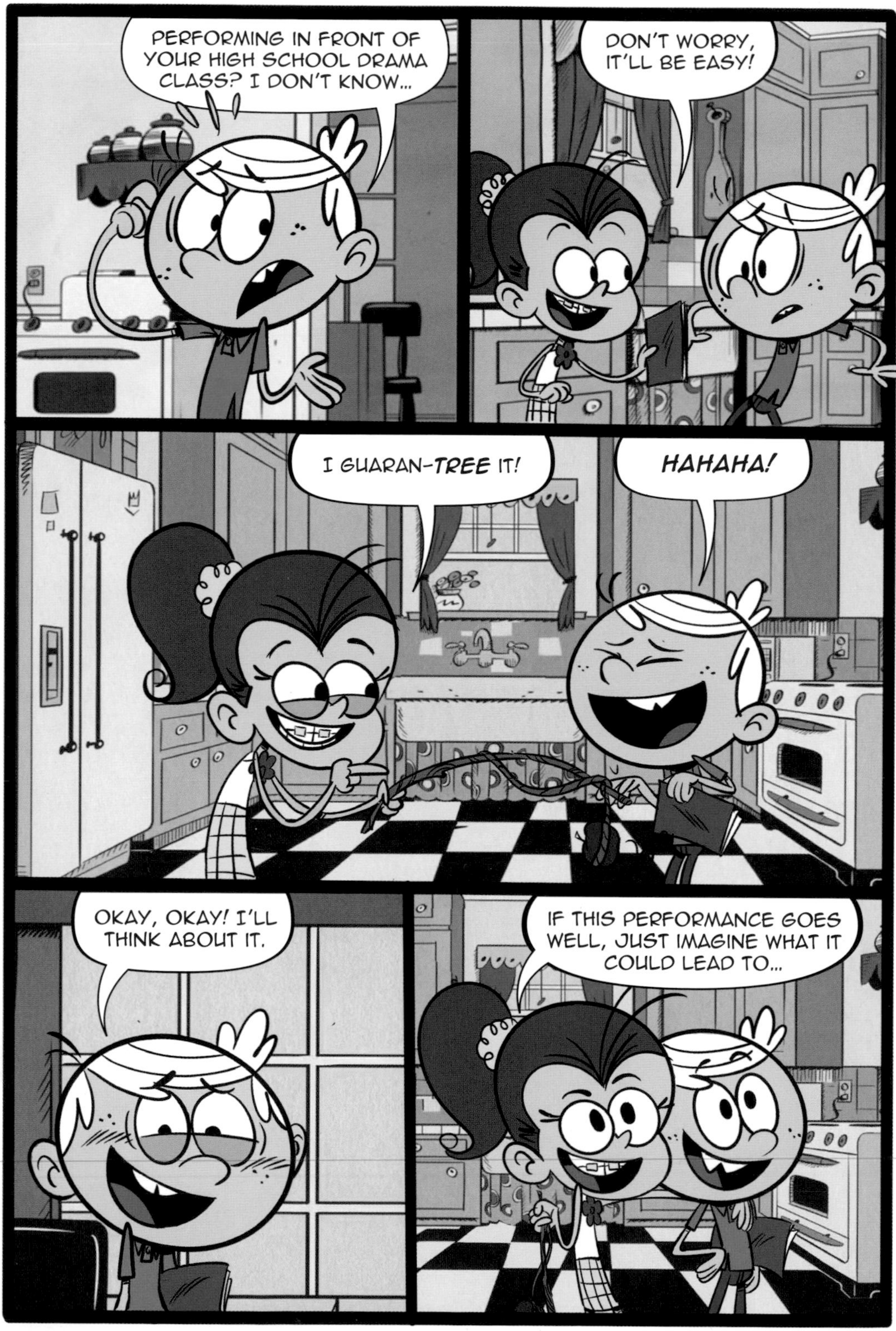
PERFORMING IN FRONT OF YOUR HIGH SCHOOL DRAMA CLASS? I DON'T KNOW...
DON'T WORRY, IT'LL BE EASY!
I GUARAN-*TREE* IT!
HAHAHA!
OKAY, OKAY! I'LL THINK ABOUT IT.
IF THIS PERFORMANCE GOES WELL, JUST IMAGINE WHAT IT COULD LEAD TO...

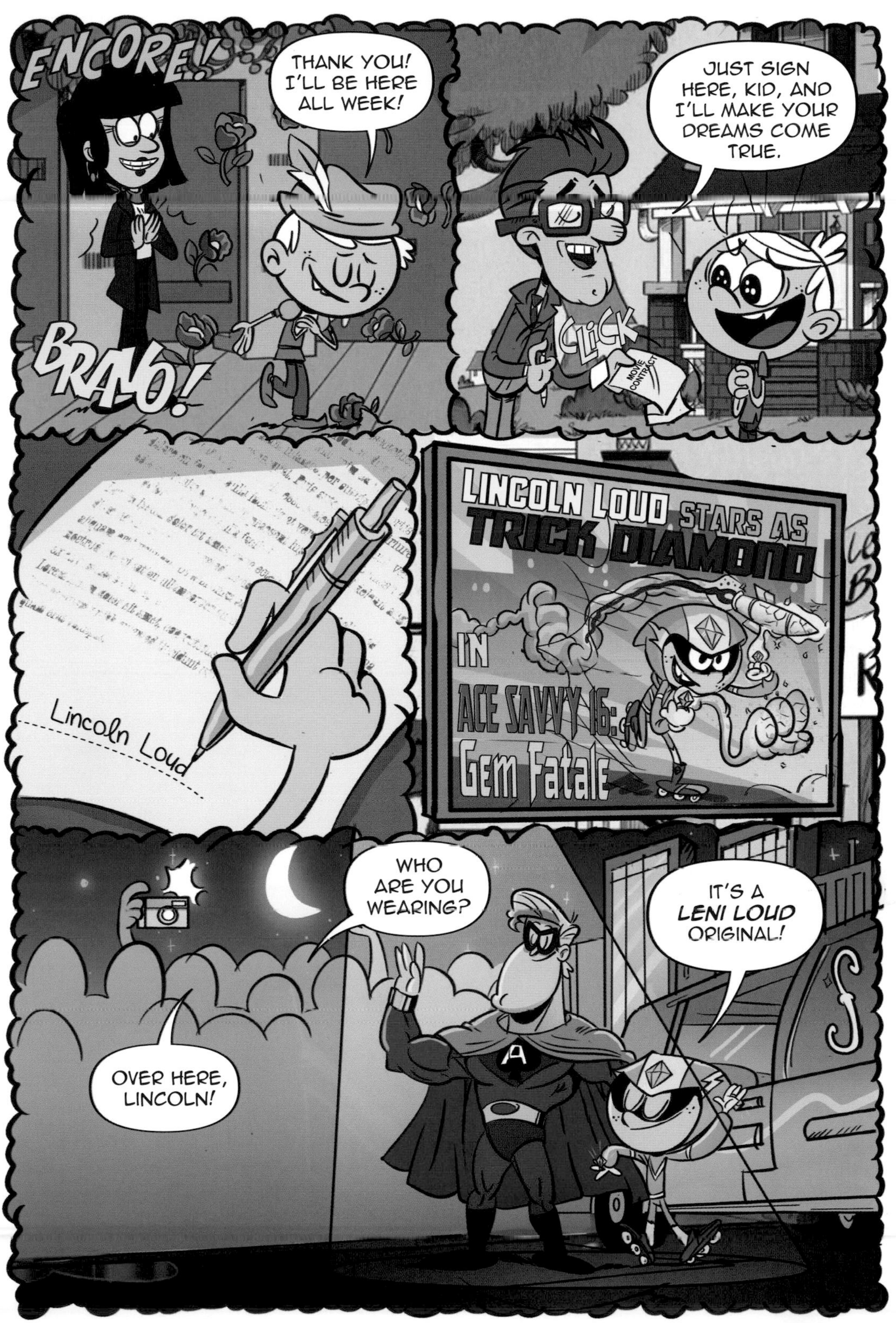
ENCORE!
THANK YOU! I'LL BE HERE ALL WEEK!
BRAVO!
JUST SIGN HERE, KID, AND I'LL MAKE YOUR DREAMS COME TRUE.
CLICK
MOVIE CONTRACT
Lincoln Loud
LINCOLN LOUD STARS AS TRICK DIAMOND IN ACE SAVVY 16: Gem Fatale
WHO ARE YOU WEARING?
IT'S A LENI LOUD ORIGINAL!
OVER HERE, LINCOLN!

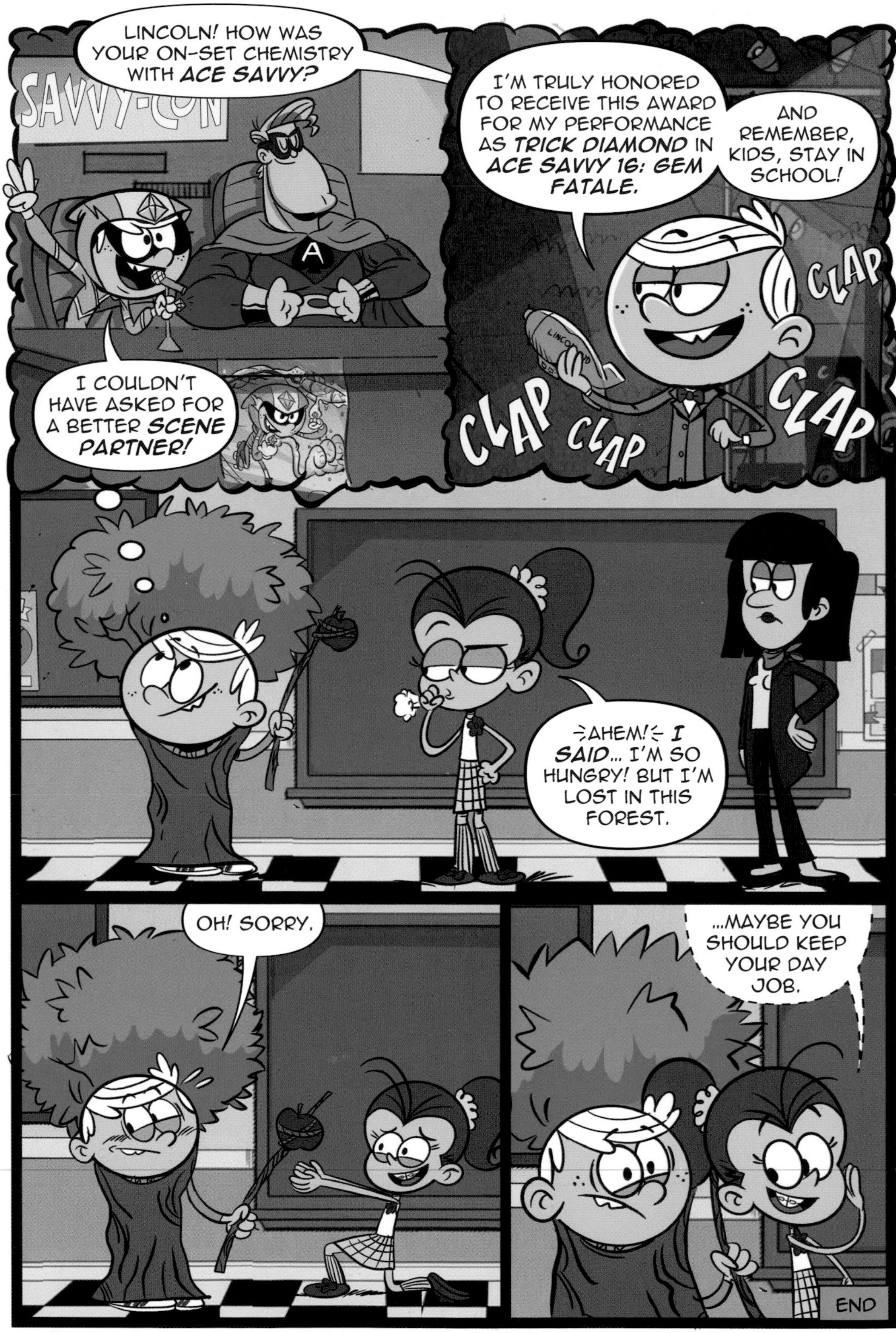
SAVVY-CON
LINCOLN! HOW WAS YOUR ON-SET CHEMISTRY WITH ACE SAVVY?
I COULDN'T HAVE ASKED FOR A BETTER SCENE PARTNER!
I'M TRULY HONORED TO RECEIVE THIS AWARD FOR MY PERFORMANCE AS TRICK DIAMOND IN ACE SAVVY 16: GEM FATALE.
AND REMEMBER, KIDS, STAY IN SCHOOL!
CLAP
CLAP
CLAP
CLAP
AHEM! I SAID... I'M SO HUNGRY! BUT I'M LOST IN THIS FOREST.
OH! SORRY.
...MAYBE YOU SHOULD KEEP YOUR DAY JOB.
END

"SURPRISE MEET AND GREET!"

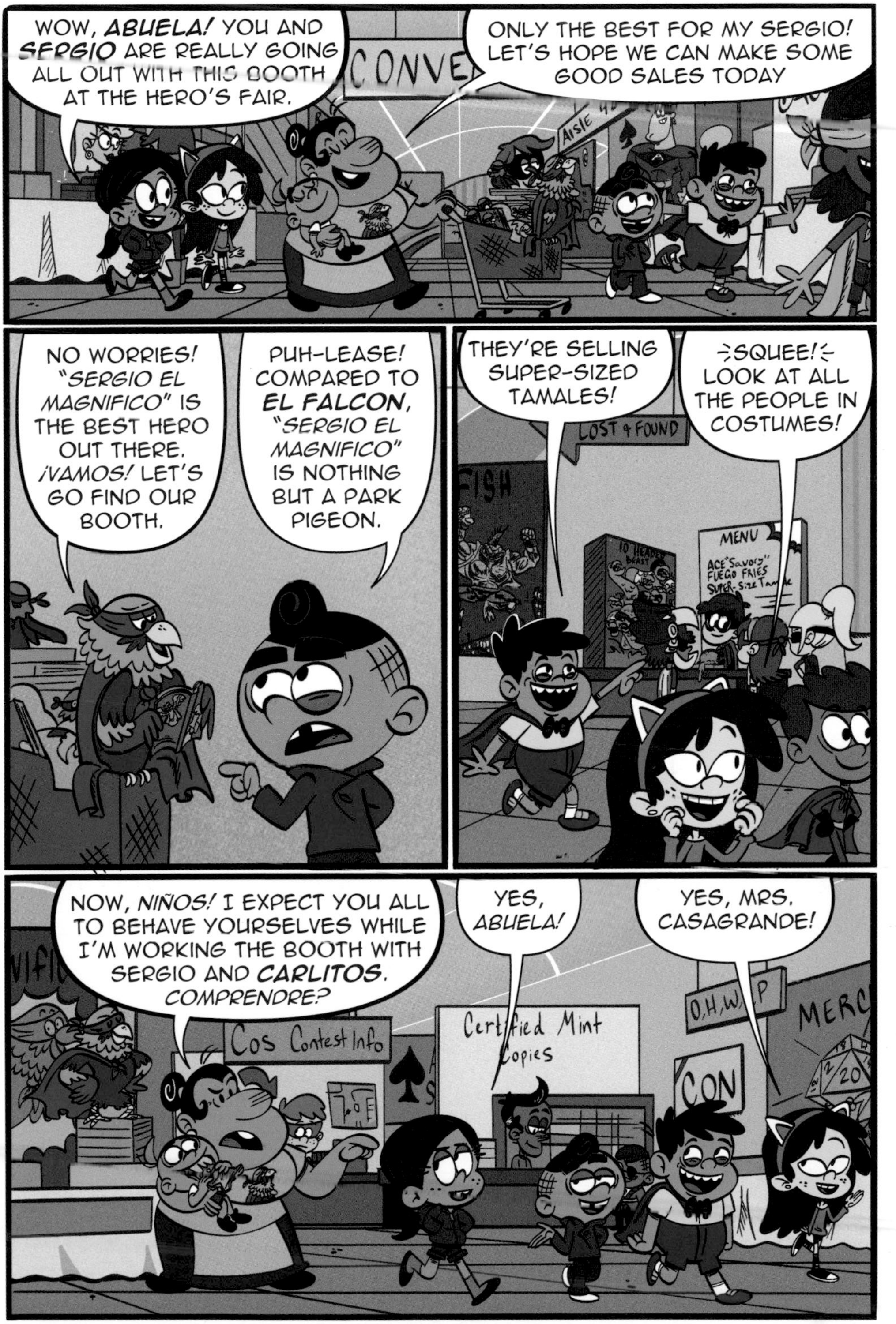

WOW, ABUELA! YOU AND SERGIO ARE REALLY GOING ALL OUT WITH THIS BOOTH AT THE HERO'S FAIR.
ONLY THE BEST FOR MY SERGIO! LET'S HOPE WE CAN MAKE SOME GOOD SALES TODAY
CONVE
AISLE
NO WORRIES! "SERGIO EL MAGNIFICO" IS THE BEST HERO OUT THERE. ¡VAMOS! LET'S GO FIND OUR BOOTH.
PUH-LEASE! COMPARED TO EL FALCON, "SERGIO EL MAGNIFICO" IS NOTHING BUT A PARK PIGEON.
THEY'RE SELLING SUPER-SIZED TAMALES!
SQUEE! LOOK AT ALL THE PEOPLE IN COSTUMES!
LOST & FOUND
FISH
MENU
NOW, NIÑOS! I EXPECT YOU ALL TO BEHAVE YOURSELVES WHILE I'M WORKING THE BOOTH WITH SERGIO AND CARLITOS. COMPRENDRE?
YES, ABUELA!
YES, MRS. CASAGRANDE!
Cos Contest Info.
Certified Mint Copies
O,H,W,P
CON
MERC

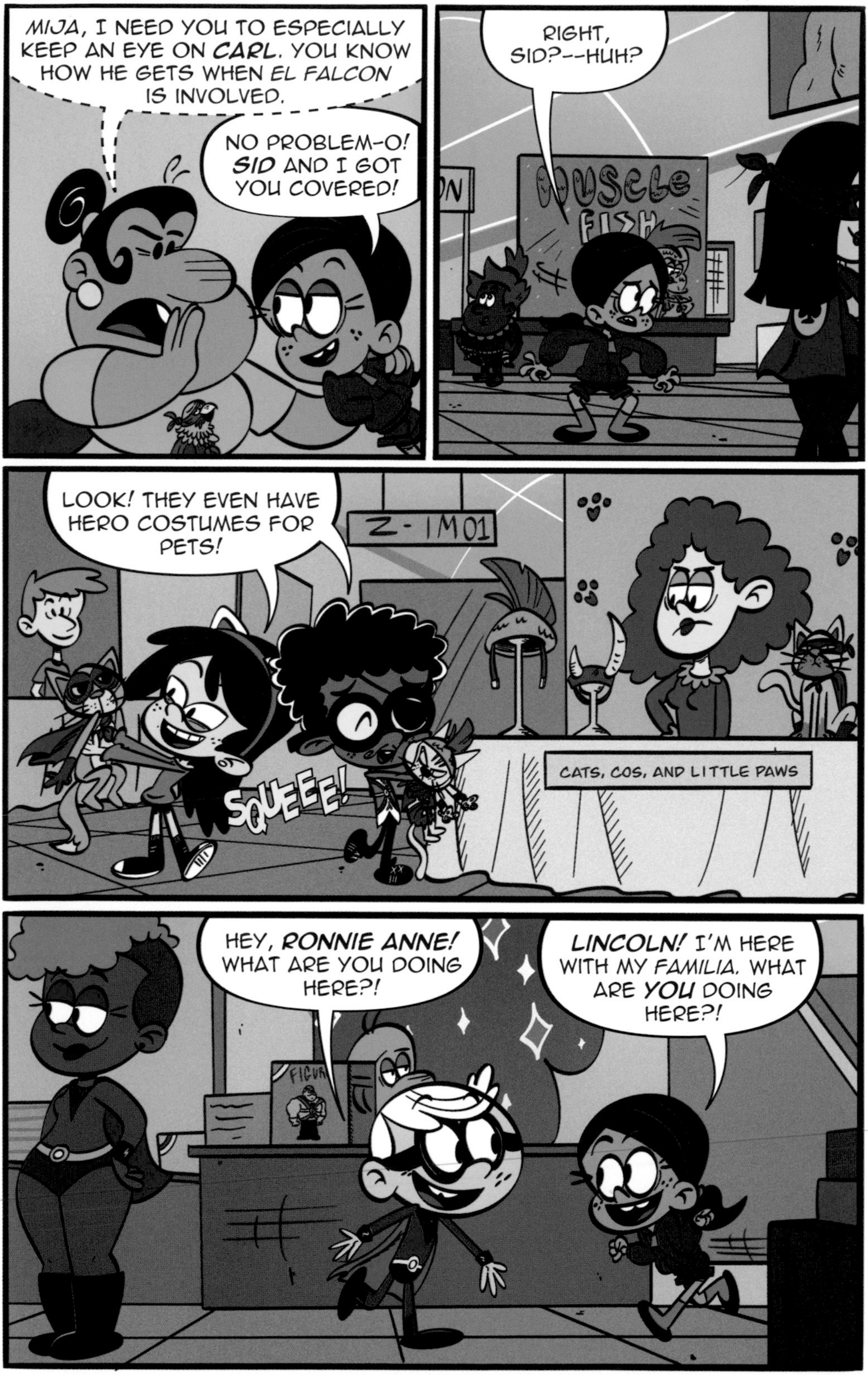
MIJA, I NEED YOU TO ESPECIALLY KEEP AN EYE ON CARL. YOU KNOW HOW HE GETS WHEN EL FALCON IS INVOLVED.
NO PROBLEM-O! SID AND I GOT YOU COVERED!
RIGHT, SID?--HUH?
MUSCLE FISH
LOOK! THEY EVEN HAVE HERO COSTUMES FOR PETS!
Z-IM01
CATS, COS, AND LITTLE PAWS
SQUEEE!
HEY, RONNIE ANNE! WHAT ARE YOU DOING HERE?!
LINCOLN! I'M HERE WITH MY FAMILIA. WHAT ARE YOU DOING HERE?!

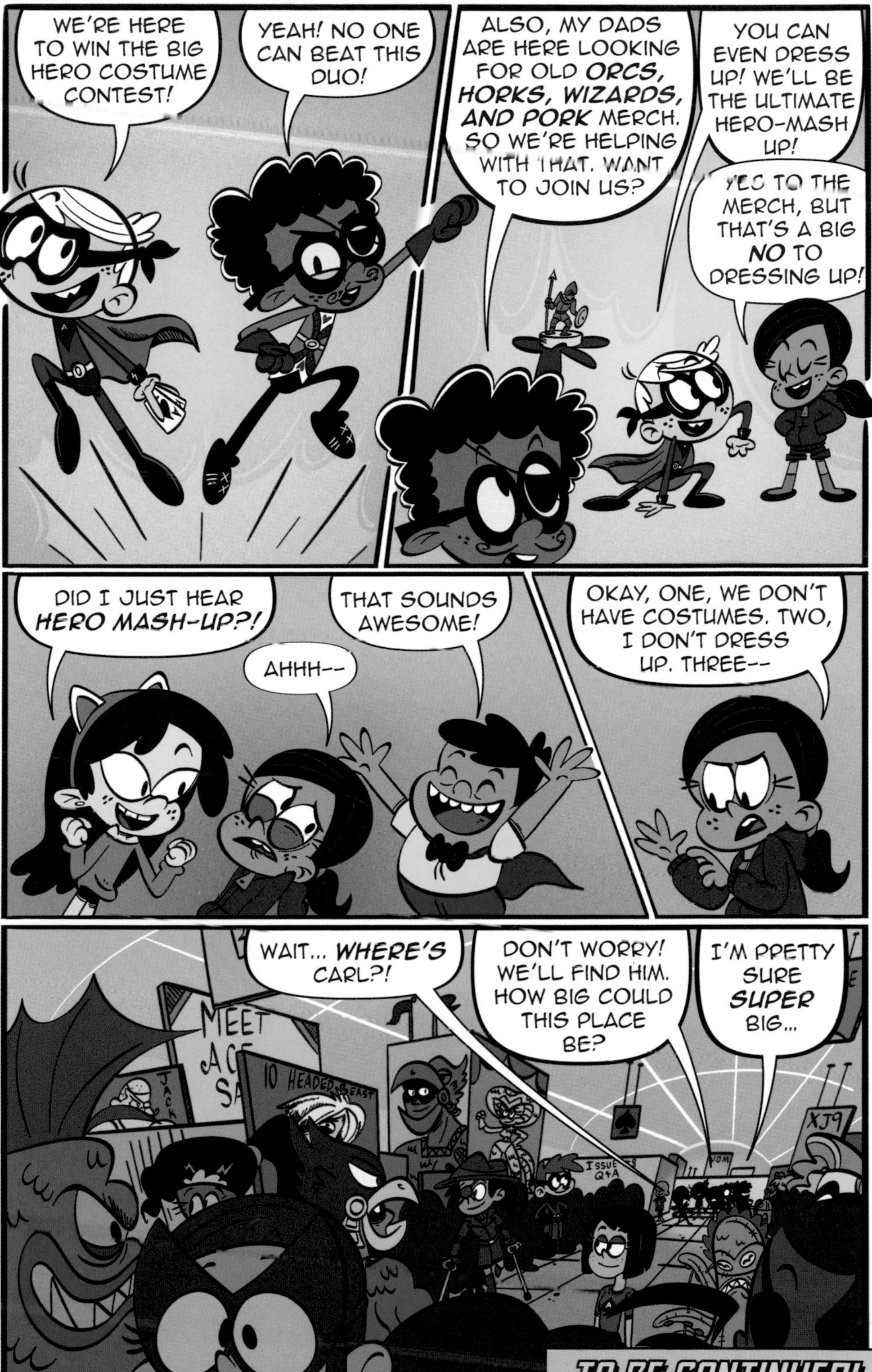
WE'RE HERE TO WIN THE BIG HERO COSTUME CONTEST!
YEAH! NO ONE CAN BEAT THIS DUO!
ALSO, MY DADS ARE HERE LOOKING FOR OLD ***ORCS, HORKS, WIZARDS, AND PORK*** MERCH. SO WE'RE HELPING WITH THAT. WANT TO JOIN US?
YOU CAN EVEN DRESS UP! WE'LL BE THE ULTIMATE HERO-MASH UP!
YES TO THE MERCH, BUT THAT'S A BIG ***NO*** TO DRESSING UP!
DID I JUST HEAR ***HERO MASH-UP?!***
AHHH--
THAT SOUNDS AWESOME!
OKAY, ONE, WE DON'T HAVE COSTUMES. TWO, I DON'T DRESS UP. THREE--
WAIT... ***WHERE'S*** CARL?!
DON'T WORRY! WE'LL FIND HIM. HOW BIG COULD THIS PLACE BE?
I'M PRETTY SURE ***SUPER*** BIG...
MEET
10 HEADED BEAST
XJ9
TO BE CONTINUED!

"COMICS, TRICKS, AND CARL AMISS!"

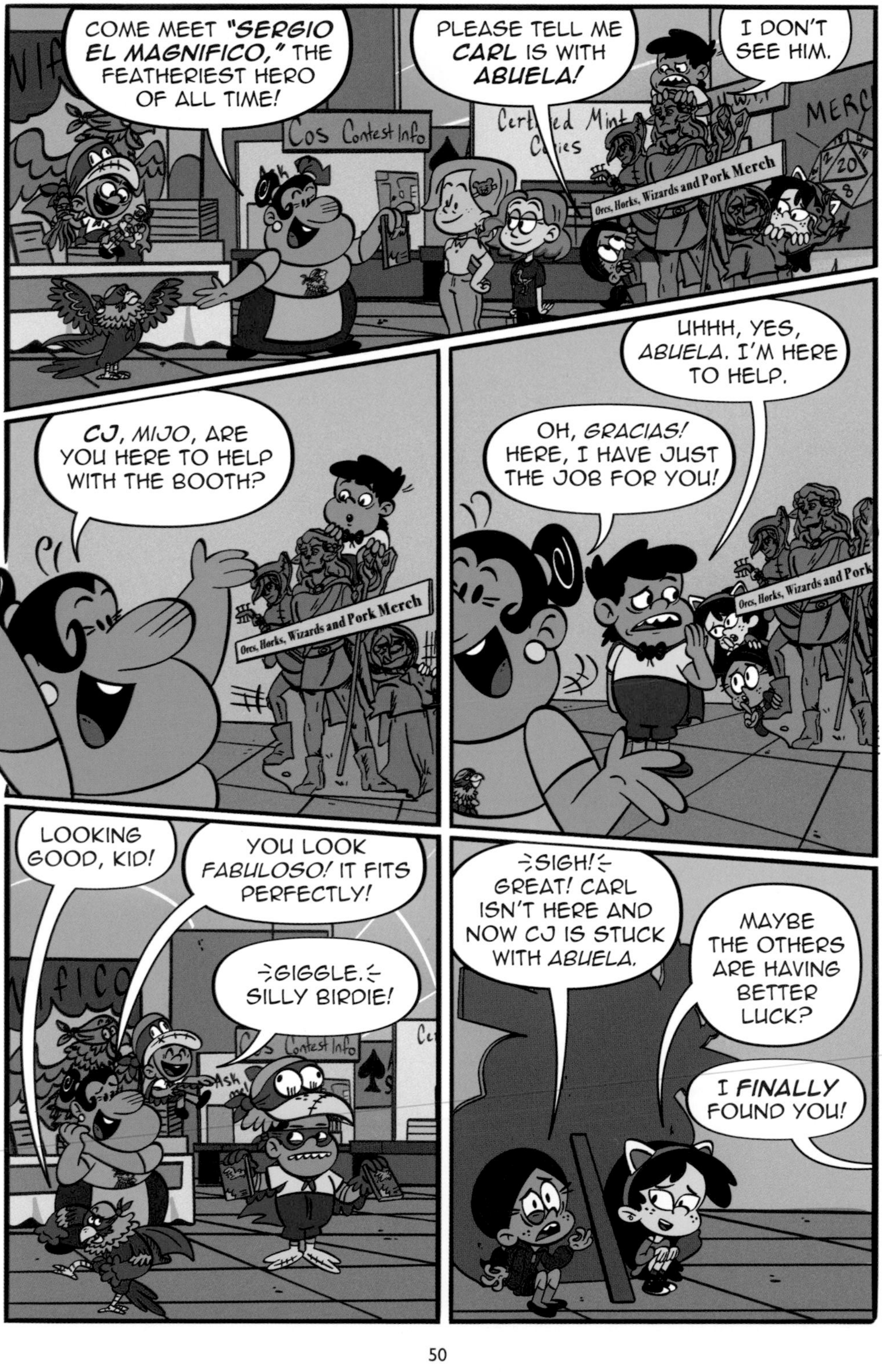
COME MEET "SERGIO EL MAGNIFICO," THE FEATHERIEST HERO OF ALL TIME!
Cos Contest Info
PLEASE TELL ME CARL IS WITH ABUELA!
I DON'T SEE HIM.
Orcs, Horks, Wizards and Pork Merch
CJ, MIJO, ARE YOU HERE TO HELP WITH THE BOOTH?
UHHH, YES, ABUELA. I'M HERE TO HELP.
OH, GRACIAS! HERE, I HAVE JUST THE JOB FOR YOU!
Orcs, Horks, Wizards and Pork Merch
Orcs, Horks, Wizards and Pork
LOOKING GOOD, KID!
YOU LOOK FABULOSO! IT FITS PERFECTLY!
GIGGLE. SILLY BIRDIE!
Cos Contest Info
SIGH! GREAT! CARL ISN'T HERE AND NOW CJ IS STUCK WITH ABUELA.
MAYBE THE OTHERS ARE HAVING BETTER LUCK?
I FINALLY FOUND YOU!

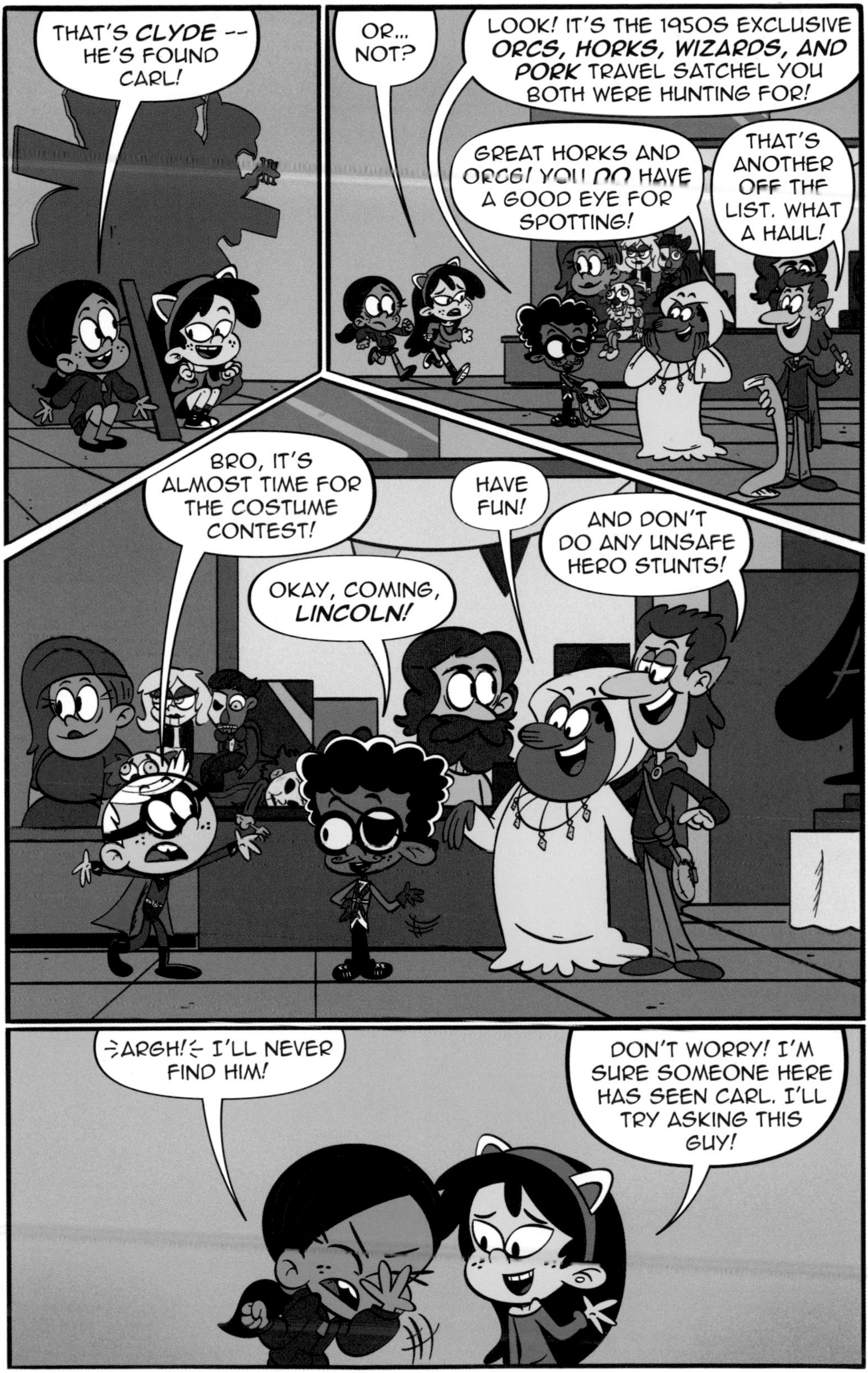

THAT'S CLYDE -- HE'S FOUND CARL!
OR... NOT?
LOOK! IT'S THE 1950S EXCLUSIVE ORCS, HORKS, WIZARDS, AND PORK TRAVEL SATCHEL YOU BOTH WERE HUNTING FOR!
GREAT HORKS AND ORCS! YOU DO HAVE A GOOD EYE FOR SPOTTING!
THAT'S ANOTHER OFF THE LIST. WHAT A HAUL!
BRO, IT'S ALMOST TIME FOR THE COSTUME CONTEST!
OKAY, COMING, LINCOLN!
HAVE FUN!
AND DON'T DO ANY UNSAFE HERO STUNTS!
ARGH! I'LL NEVER FIND HIM!
DON'T WORRY! I'M SURE SOMEONE HERE HAS SEEN CARL. I'LL TRY ASKING THIS GUY!

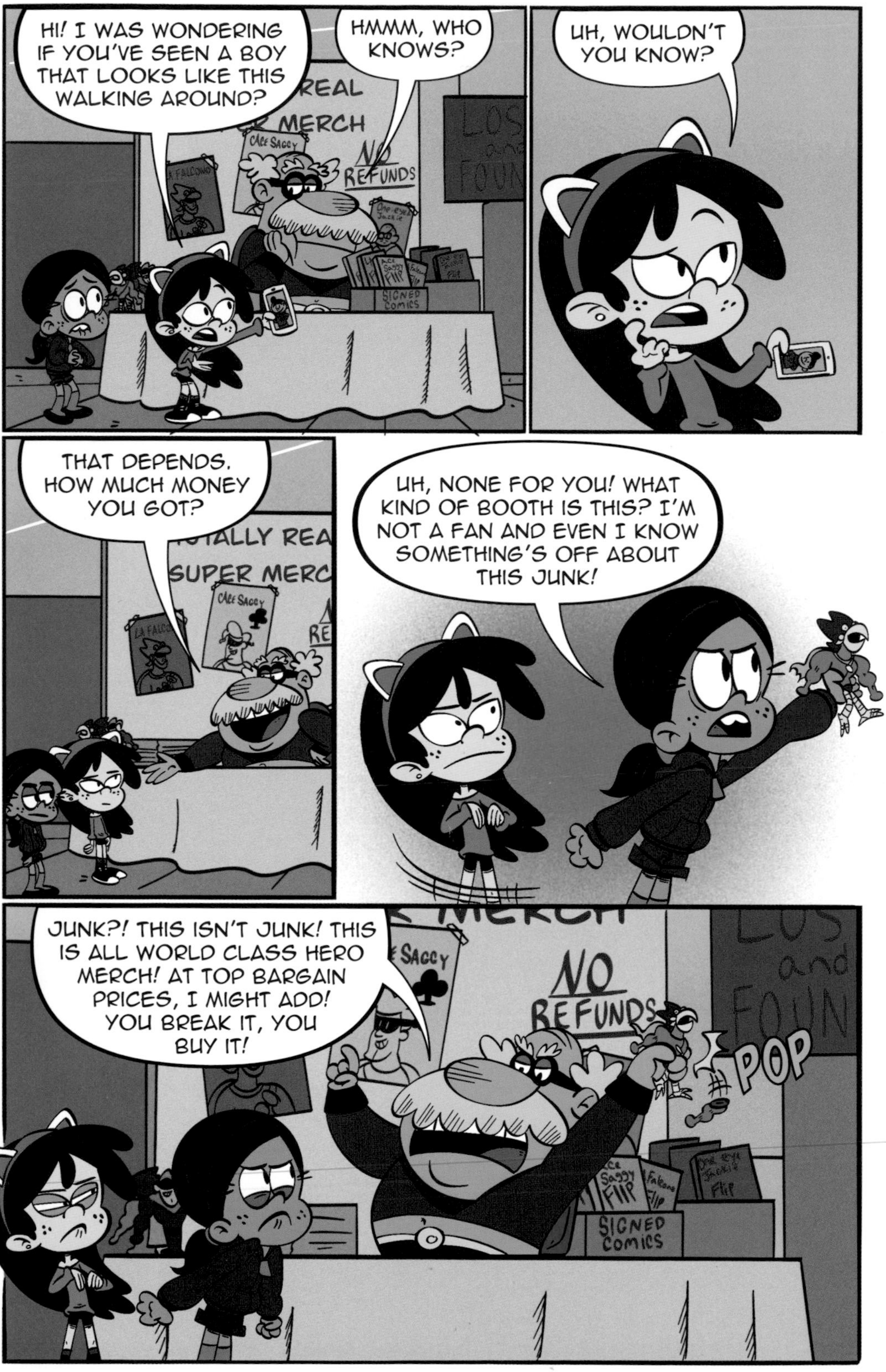

HI! I WAS WONDERING IF YOU'VE SEEN A BOY THAT LOOKS LIKE THIS WALKING AROUND?
HMMM, WHO KNOWS?
NO REFUNDS
SIGNED COMICS
UH, WOULDN'T YOU KNOW?
THAT DEPENDS. HOW MUCH MONEY YOU GOT?
UH, NONE FOR YOU! WHAT KIND OF BOOTH IS THIS? I'M NOT A FAN AND EVEN I KNOW SOMETHING'S OFF ABOUT THIS JUNK!
JUNK?! THIS ISN'T JUNK! THIS IS ALL WORLD CLASS HERO MERCH! AT TOP BARGAIN PRICES, I MIGHT ADD! YOU BREAK IT, YOU BUY IT!
NO REFUNDS
POP
SIGNED COMICS

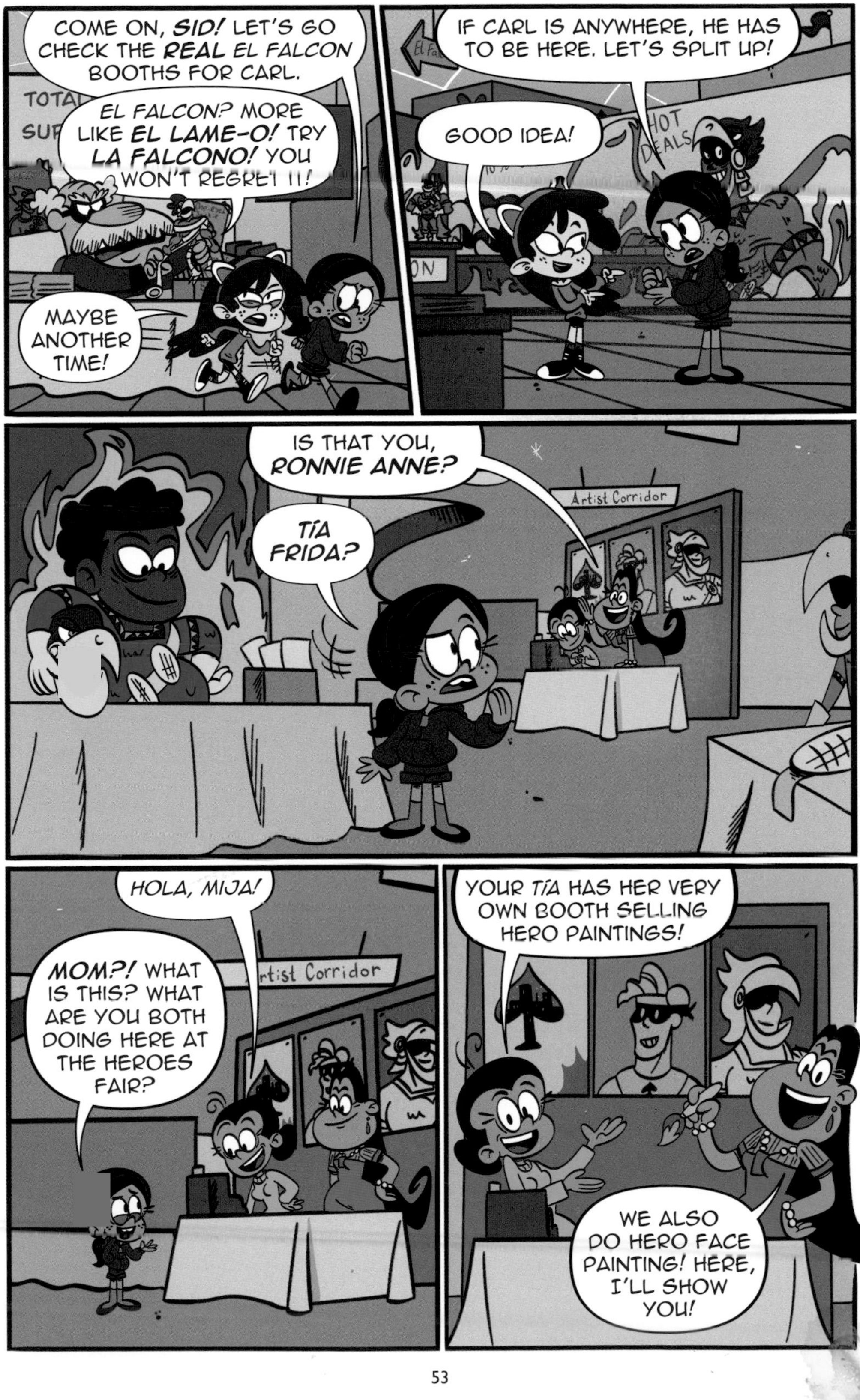
COME ON, SID! LET'S GO CHECK THE REAL EL FALCON BOOTHS FOR CARL.
EL FALCON? MORE LIKE EL LAME-O! TRY LA FALCONO! YOU WON'T REGRET IT!
MAYBE ANOTHER TIME!
IF CARL IS ANYWHERE, HE HAS TO BE HERE. LET'S SPLIT UP!
GOOD IDEA!
HOT DEALS
IS THAT YOU, RONNIE ANNE?
TÍA FRIDA?
Artist Corridor
HOLA, MIJA!
MOM?! WHAT IS THIS? WHAT ARE YOU BOTH DOING HERE AT THE HEROES FAIR?
Artist Corridor
YOUR TÍA HAS HER VERY OWN BOOTH SELLING HERO PAINTINGS!
WE ALSO DO HERO FACE PAINTING! HERE, I'LL SHOW YOU!

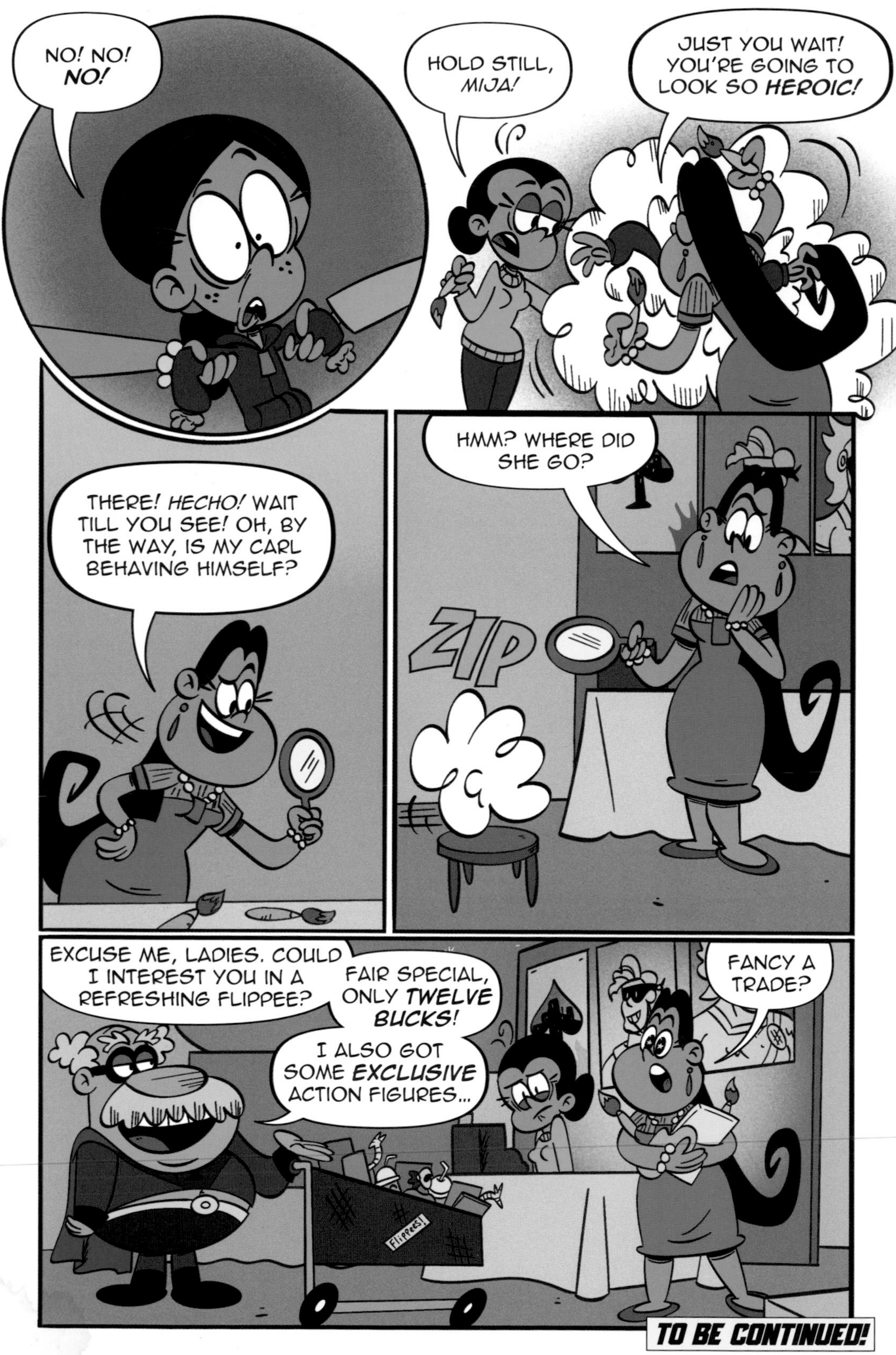
NO! NO! NO!
HOLD STILL, MIJA!
JUST YOU WAIT! YOU'RE GOING TO LOOK SO HEROIC!
THERE! HECHO! WAIT TILL YOU SEE! OH, BY THE WAY, IS MY CARL BEHAVING HIMSELF?
HMM? WHERE DID SHE GO?
ZIP
EXCUSE ME, LADIES. COULD I INTEREST YOU IN A REFRESHING FLIPPEE?
FAIR SPECIAL, ONLY TWELVE BUCKS!
I ALSO GOT SOME EXCLUSIVE ACTION FIGURES...
FANCY A TRADE?
FLIPPEES!
TO BE CONTINUED!

"DRESSED TO POSE!"

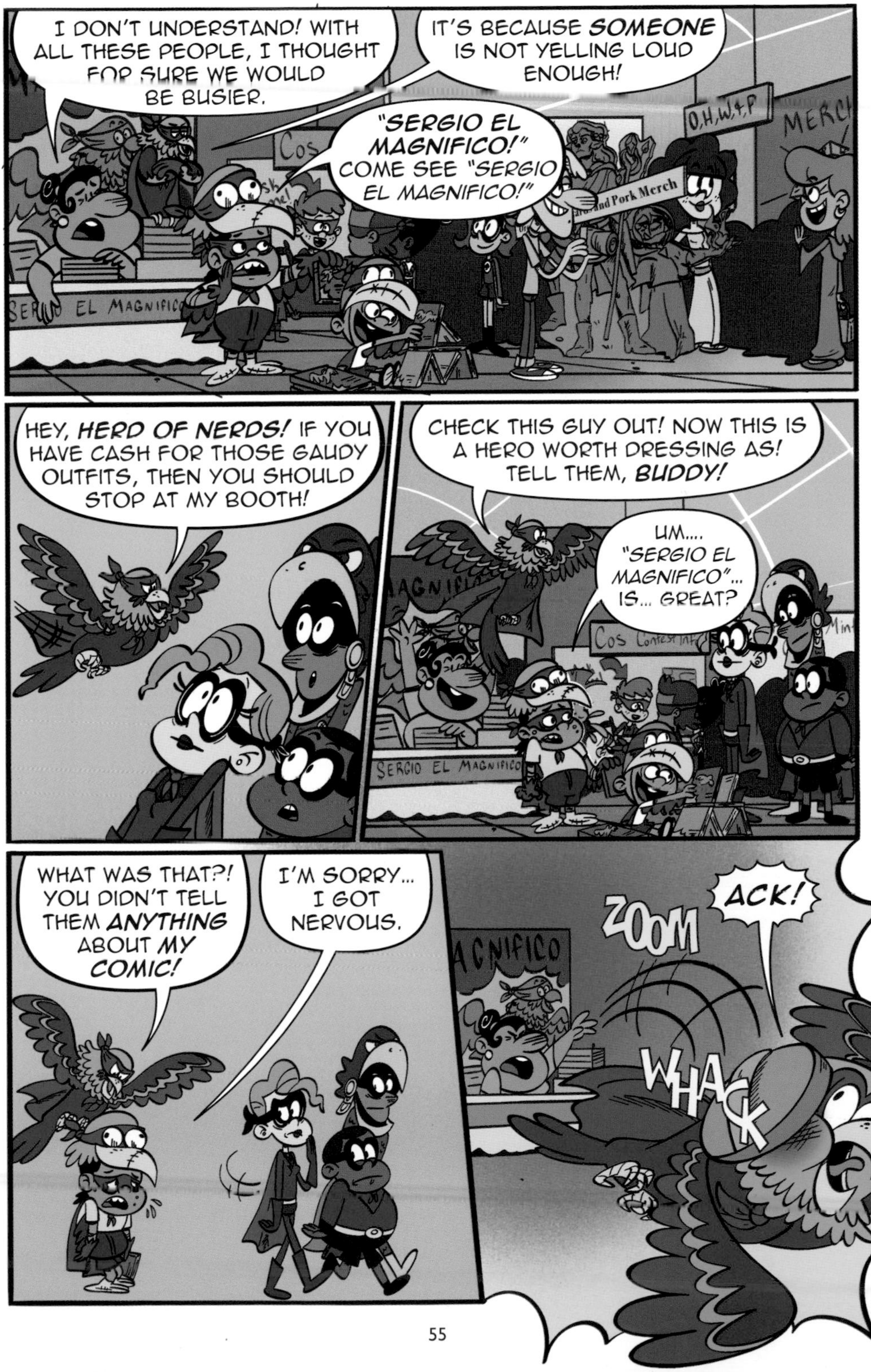

I DON'T UNDERSTAND! WITH ALL THESE PEOPLE, I THOUGHT FOR SURE WE WOULD BE BUSIER.
IT'S BECAUSE SOMEONE IS NOT YELLING LOUD ENOUGH!
"SERGIO EL MAGNIFICO!" COME SEE "SERGIO EL MAGNIFICO!"
O.H.W.&P
MERCH
Pork Merch
SERGIO EL MAGNIFICO
HEY, HERD OF NERDS! IF YOU HAVE CASH FOR THOSE GAUDY OUTFITS, THEN YOU SHOULD STOP AT MY BOOTH!
CHECK THIS GUY OUT! NOW THIS IS A HERO WORTH DRESSING AS! TELL THEM, BUDDY!
UM.... "SERGIO EL MAGNIFICO"... IS... GREAT?
Cos Contest Info
SERGIO EL MAGNIFICO
WHAT WAS THAT?! YOU DIDN'T TELL THEM ANYTHING ABOUT MY COMIC!
I'M SORRY... I GOT NERVOUS.
ZOOM
ACK!
MAGNIFICO
WHACK

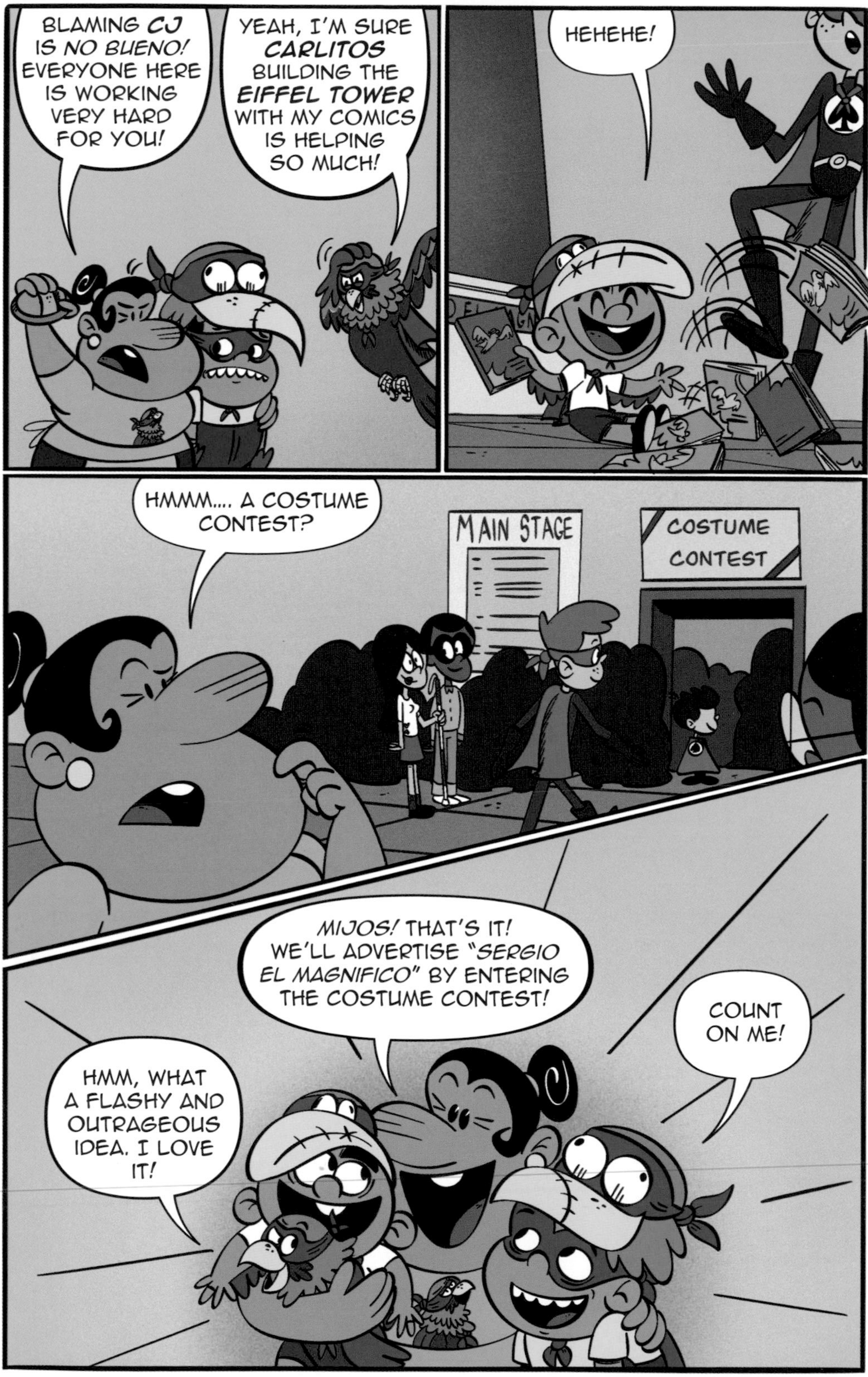
BLAMING *CJ* IS *NO BUENO!* EVERYONE HERE IS WORKING VERY HARD FOR YOU!
YEAH, I'M SURE **CARLITOS** BUILDING THE ***EIFFEL TOWER*** WITH MY COMICS IS HELPING SO MUCH!
HEHEHE!
HMMM.... A COSTUME CONTEST?
MAIN STAGE
COSTUME CONTEST
MIJOS! THAT'S IT! WE'LL ADVERTISE "*SERGIO EL MAGNIFICO*" BY ENTERING THE COSTUME CONTEST!
COUNT ON ME!
HMM, WHAT A FLASHY AND OUTRAGEOUS IDEA. I LOVE IT!

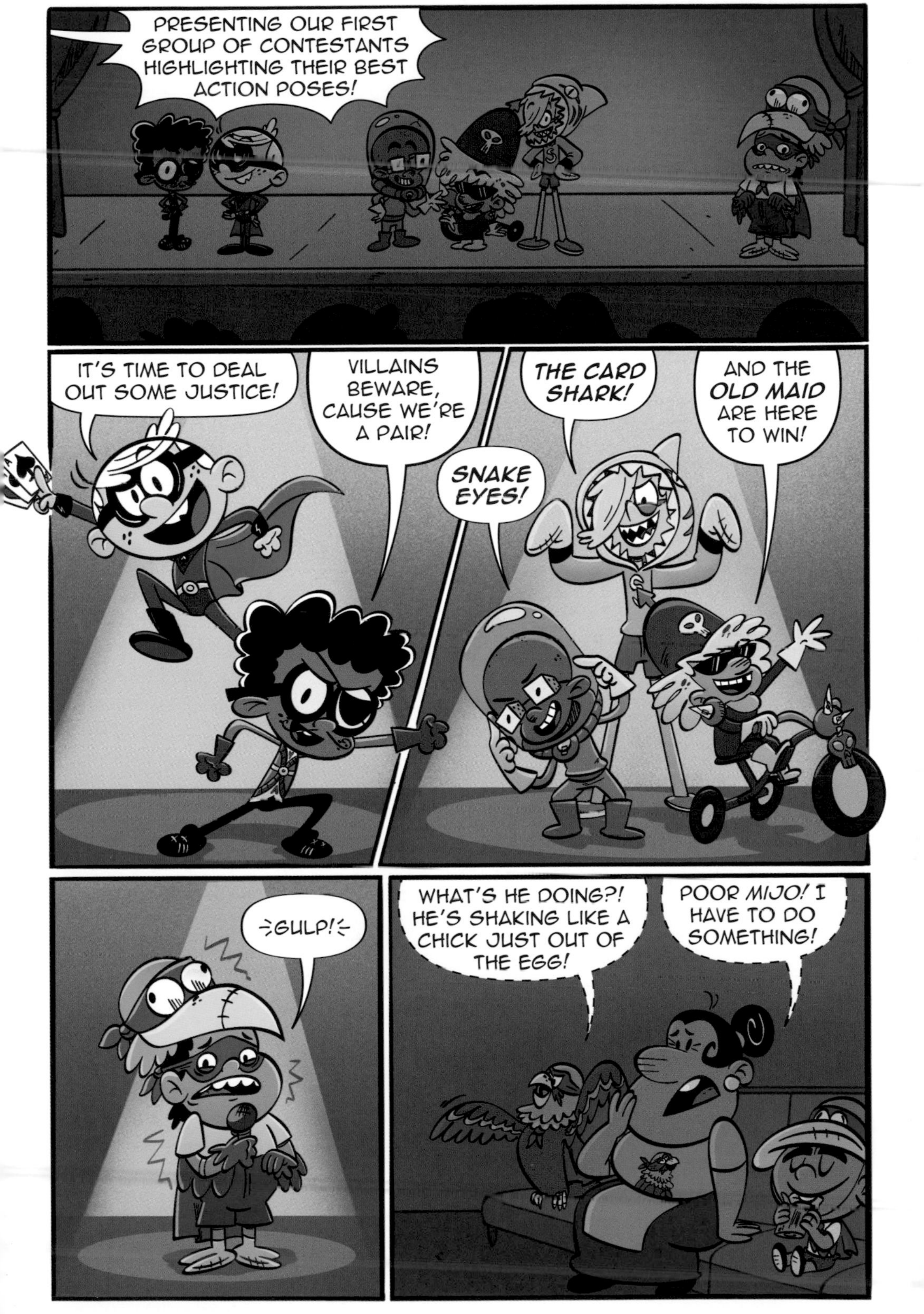
PRESENTING OUR FIRST GROUP OF CONTESTANTS HIGHLIGHTING THEIR BEST ACTION POSES!
IT'S TIME TO DEAL OUT SOME JUSTICE!
VILLAINS BEWARE, CAUSE WE'RE A PAIR!
THE CARD SHARK!
SNAKE EYES!
AND THE OLD MAID ARE HERE TO WIN!
GULP!
WHAT'S HE DOING?! HE'S SHAKING LIKE A CHICK JUST OUT OF THE EGG!
POOR MIJO! I HAVE TO DO SOMETHING!

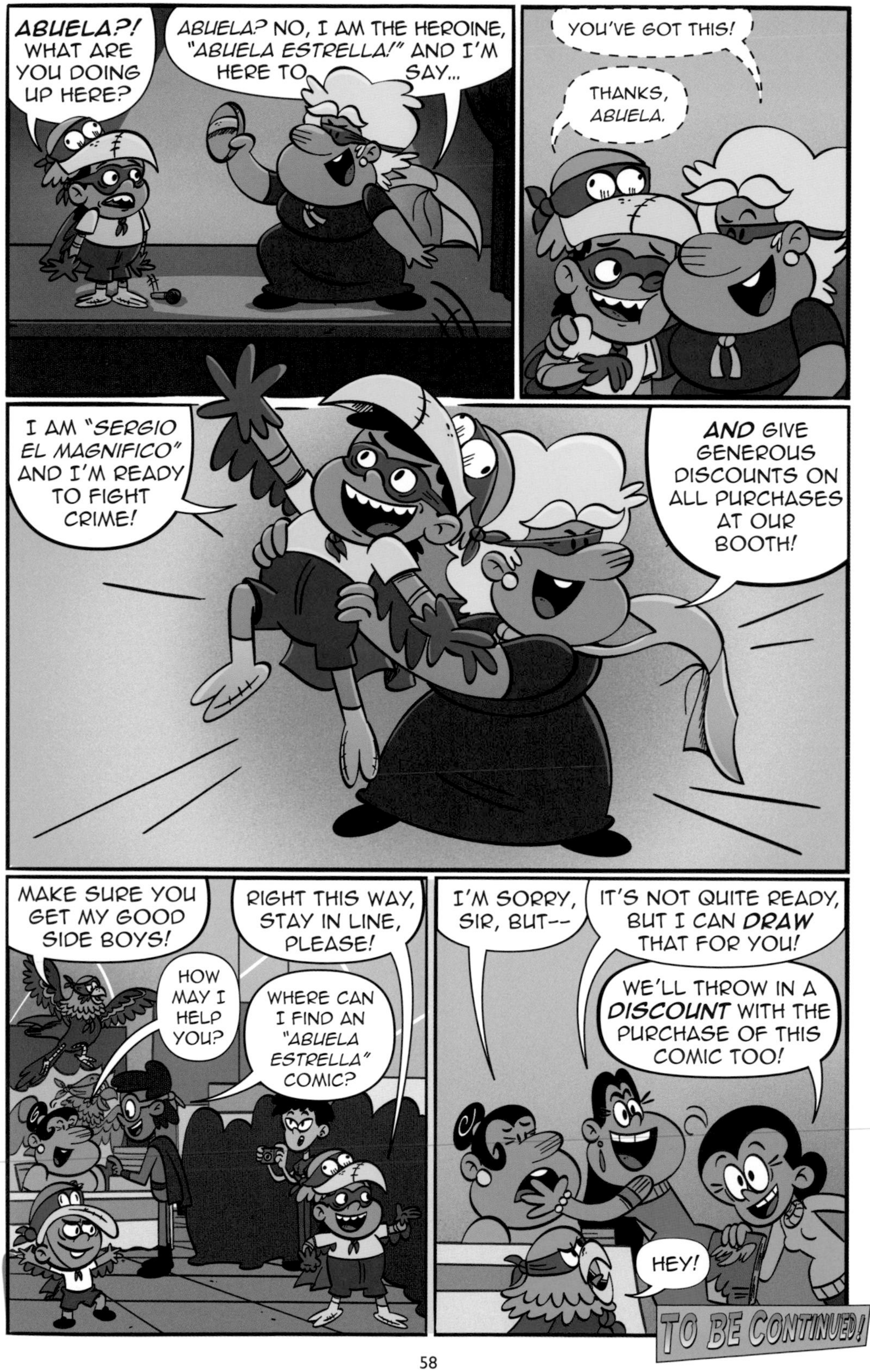
ABUELA?! WHAT ARE YOU DOING UP HERE?
ABUELA? NO, I AM THE HEROINE, "ABUELA ESTRELLA!" AND I'M HERE TO SAY...
YOU'VE GOT THIS!
THANKS, ABUELA.
I AM "SERGIO EL MAGNIFICO" AND I'M READY TO FIGHT CRIME!
AND GIVE GENEROUS DISCOUNTS ON ALL PURCHASES AT OUR BOOTH!
MAKE SURE YOU GET MY GOOD SIDE BOYS!
RIGHT THIS WAY, STAY IN LINE, PLEASE!
HOW MAY I HELP YOU?
WHERE CAN I FIND AN "ABUELA ESTRELLA" COMIC?
I'M SORRY, SIR, BUT--
IT'S NOT QUITE READY, BUT I CAN DRAW THAT FOR YOU!
WE'LL THROW IN A DISCOUNT WITH THE PURCHASE OF THIS COMIC TOO!
HEY!
TO BE CONTINUED!

ACE SAVVY Vs.... CARL?!

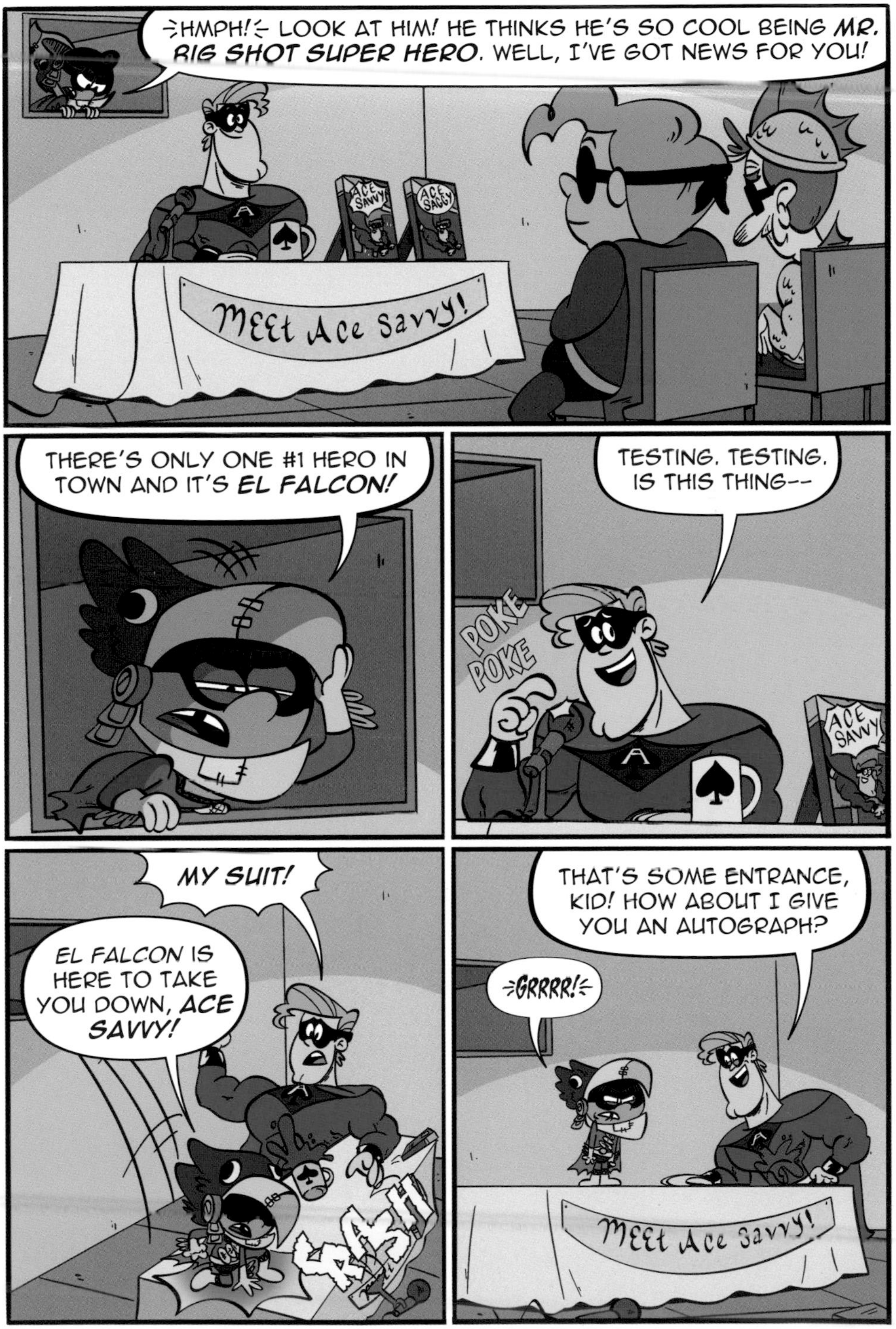
HMPH! LOOK AT HIM! HE THINKS HE'S SO COOL BEING MR. BIG SHOT SUPER HERO. WELL, I'VE GOT NEWS FOR YOU!
ACE SAVVY
ACE SAVVY
MEEt Ace Savvy!
THERE'S ONLY ONE #1 HERO IN TOWN AND IT'S EL FALCON!
TESTING. TESTING. IS THIS THING--
POKE
POKE
ACE SAVVY
MY SUIT!
EL FALCON IS HERE TO TAKE YOU DOWN, ACE SAVVY!
CRASH!
THAT'S SOME ENTRANCE, KID! HOW ABOUT I GIVE YOU AN AUTOGRAPH?
GRRRR!
MEEt Ace Savvy!

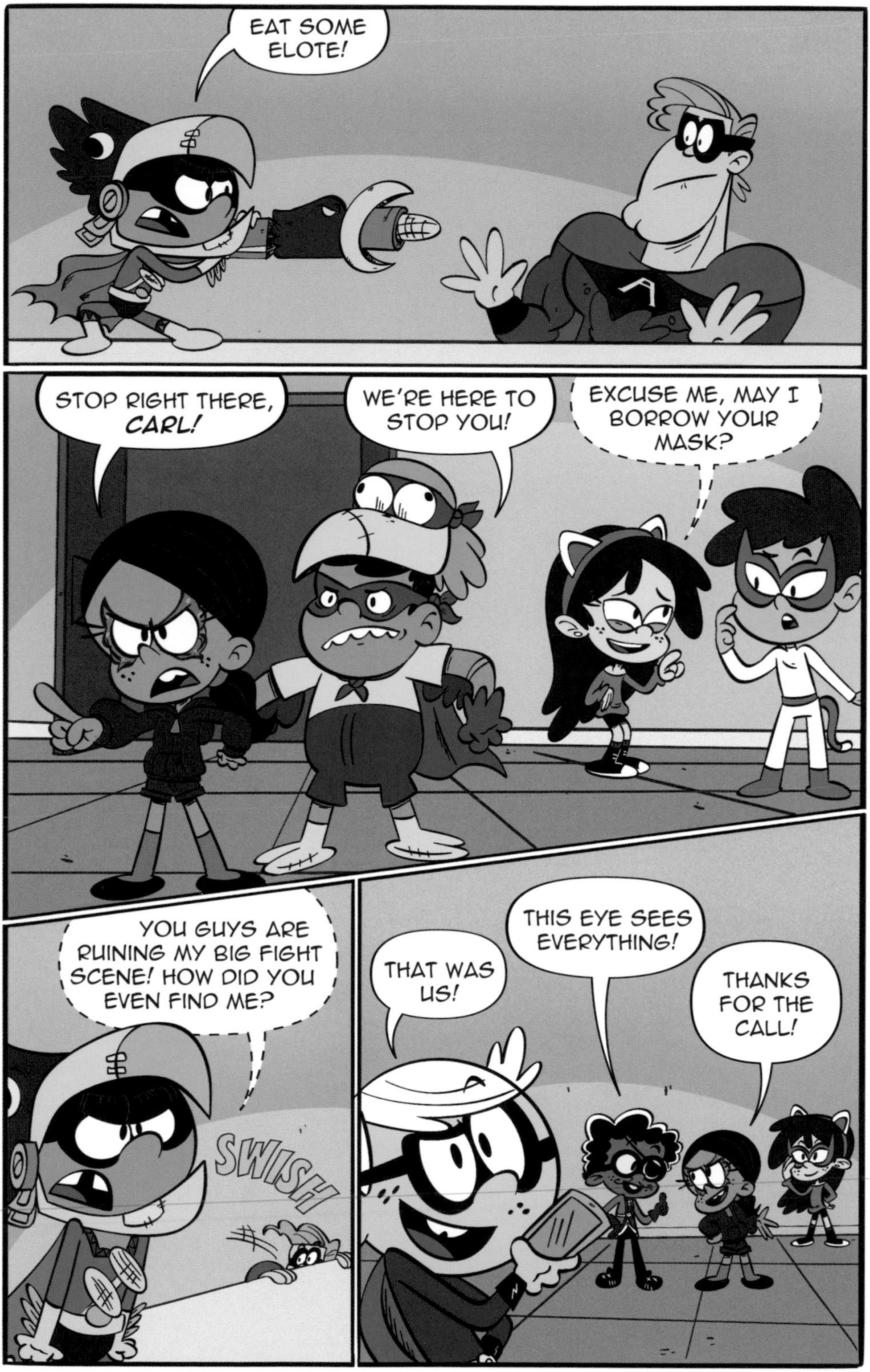
EAT SOME ELOTE!
STOP RIGHT THERE, CARL!
WE'RE HERE TO STOP YOU!
EXCUSE ME, MAY I BORROW YOUR MASK?
YOU GUYS ARE RUINING MY BIG FIGHT SCENE! HOW DID YOU EVEN FIND ME?
SWISH
THAT WAS US!
THIS EYE SEES EVERYTHING!
THANKS FOR THE CALL!

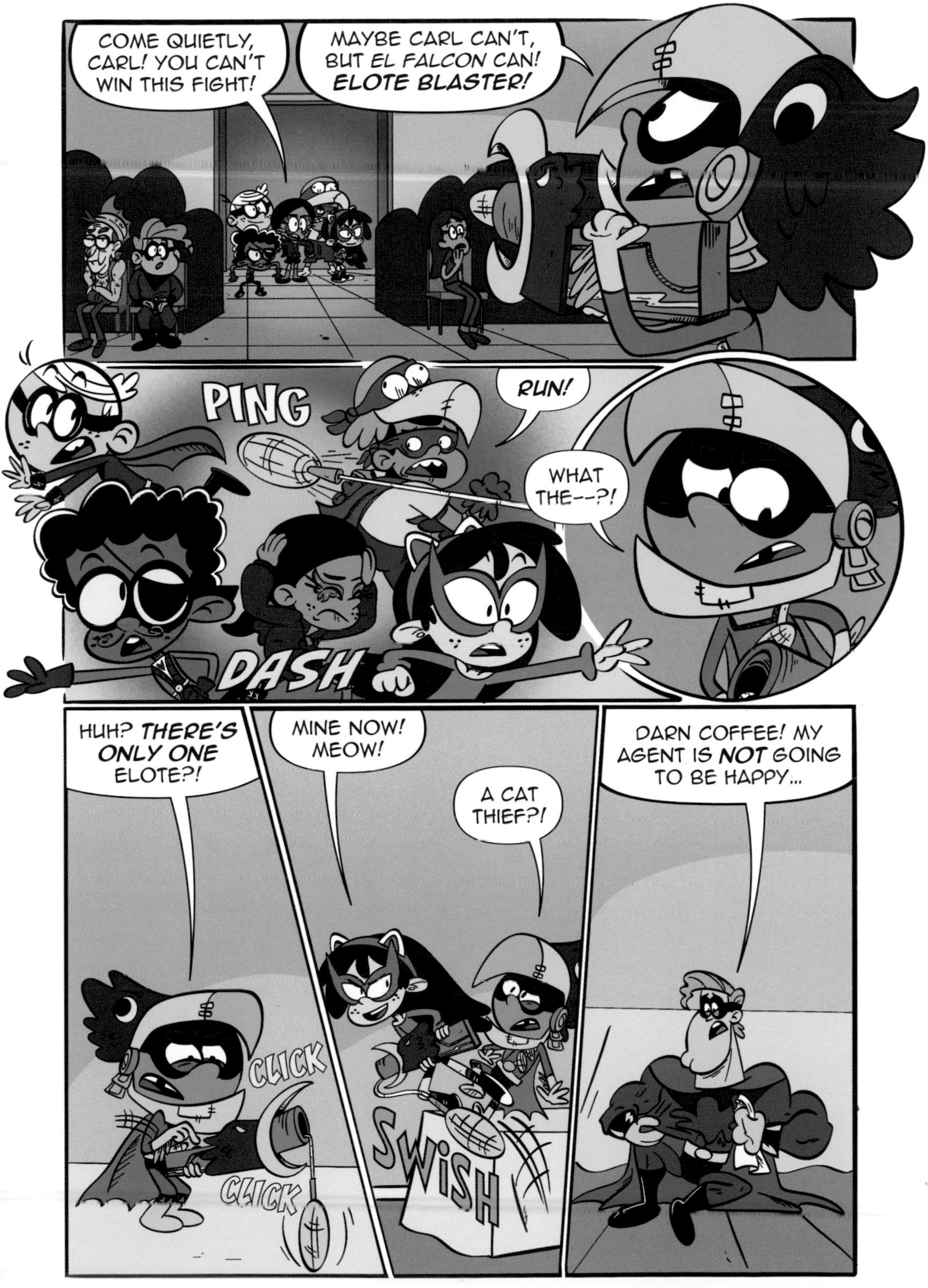
COME QUIETLY, CARL! YOU CAN'T WIN THIS FIGHT!
MAYBE CARL CAN'T, BUT *EL FALCON* CAN! ***ELOTE BLASTER!***
PING
RUN!
WHAT THE--?!
DASH
HUH? ***THERE'S ONLY ONE*** ELOTE?!
CLICK
CLICK
MINE NOW! MEOW!
A CAT THIEF?!
SWISH
DARN COFFEE! MY AGENT IS ***NOT*** GOING TO BE HAPPY...

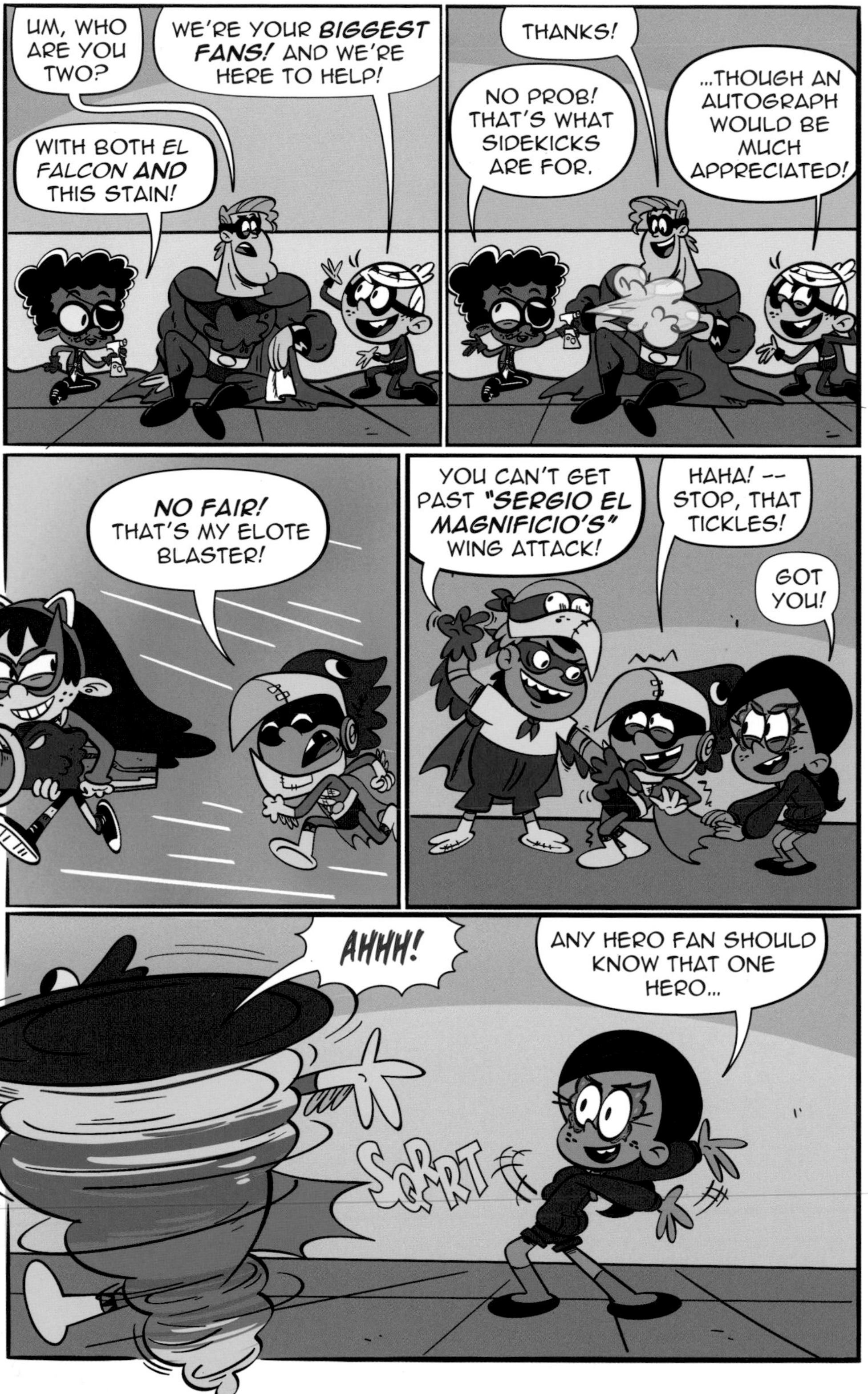
UM, WHO ARE YOU TWO?
WE'RE YOUR BIGGEST FANS! AND WE'RE HERE TO HELP!
WITH BOTH EL FALCON AND THIS STAIN!
THANKS!
NO PROB! THAT'S WHAT SIDEKICKS ARE FOR.
...THOUGH AN AUTOGRAPH WOULD BE MUCH APPRECIATED!
NO FAIR! THAT'S MY ELOTE BLASTER!
YOU CAN'T GET PAST "SERGIO EL MAGNIFICIO'S" WING ATTACK!
HAHA! -- STOP, THAT TICKLES!
GOT YOU!
AHHH!
ANY HERO FAN SHOULD KNOW THAT ONE HERO...
SQRRT

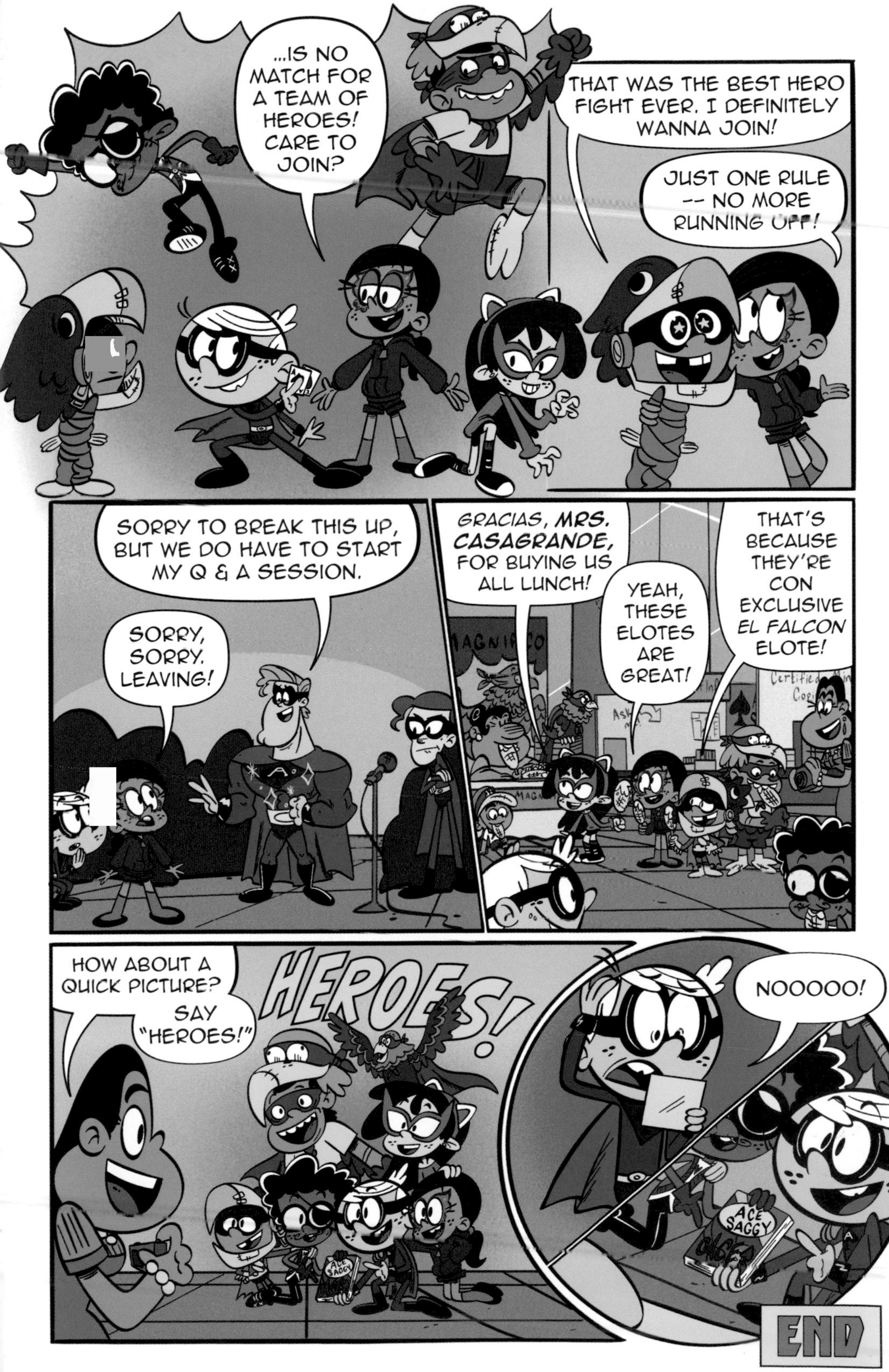
...IS NO MATCH FOR A TEAM OF HEROES! CARE TO JOIN?
THAT WAS THE BEST HERO FIGHT EVER. I DEFINITELY WANNA JOIN!
JUST ONE RULE -- NO MORE RUNNING OFF!
SORRY TO BREAK THIS UP, BUT WE DO HAVE TO START MY Q & A SESSION.
SORRY, SORRY. LEAVING!
GRACIAS, **MRS. CASAGRANDE,** FOR BUYING US ALL LUNCH!
YEAH, THESE ELOTES ARE GREAT!
THAT'S BECAUSE THEY'RE CON EXCLUSIVE *EL FALCON* ELOTE!
HOW ABOUT A QUICK PICTURE?
SAY "HEROES!"
HEROES!
NOOOOO!
ACE SAGGY
END

WATCH OUT FOR PAPERCUTZ

Welcome to the pulse-pounding premiere volume of THE LOUD HOUSE SUPER SPECIAL brought to you by Papercutz, the mild-mannered folks dedicated to publishing great graphic novels for all ages. I'm Jim Salicrup, the Papercutz Editor-in-Chief by day and Super-Hero at night (in my dreams), here to talk about the other super-powered characters that Papercutz publishes...

The first, not just alphabetically, is a shrewd little warrior with a keen intelligence named ASTERIX. While not as well known (yet!) in America as he is everywhere else in the world, ASTERIX, created by René Goscinny and Albert Uderzo, is as popular as other heroes, especially in Europe. ASTERIX's adventures are set in the year 50 BC, and his main mission is defending his little village from the Roman Empire. How's that possible? He gets superhuman strength from a magic potion that the village's venerable druid, Panoramix, prepares. While ASTERIX doesn't have a secret identity or skin-tight costume, he does have a sidekick, Obelix. Their comedic adventures have been thrilling fans for over 60 years and Papercutz is proud to publish this comic art classic graphic novel series in North America.

Then there's ASTRO MOUSE AND LIGHT BULB, by Fermín Solís, about a pair of space-faring super-heroes and their incredible (and funny) adventures. While Papercutz publishes graphic novels featuring cats (CAT & CAT, BRINA THE CAT, etc.), we also publish graphic novels featuring mice—GERONIMO STILTON REPORTER, and ASTRO MOUSE AND LIGHT BULB. While Geronimo is certainly a heroic character, he's not quite a super-hero. But ASTRO MOUSE is, and so is his sidekick, a sentient LIGHT BULB. There's also a lovable character named CACA as part of the regular cast. Their inter-stella exploits have to be seen to still not be believed, and we highly recommend checking out this over-the-top fun series.

BENNY BREAKIRON is the creation of Peyo, the same cartoonist that created the stars of Nickelodeon's hit TV series, The Smurfs. Papercutz and Abrams both publish those little blue people. Papercutz published several BENNY BREAKIRON graphic novels, but now BENNY appears in every other volume of THE SMURFS TALES. Benny is a super-strong French boy, except when he catches cold!

LOLA'S SUPER CLUB, by Christine Beigel and Pierre Fouillet, is about a young girl with an incredible imagination—or is it? She imagines she and her toys and pet cat (another cat!) are super-heroes, and that her dad is master super-spy, James Blond. Is it just her imagination or is it possible she really is a super-hero? Her adventures are just as crazy as ASTRO MOUSE AND LIGHT BULB's, so, who knows?

THE MYTHICS are a team of young super-heroes, in a series created by a team of super-comics-creators: Patrick Sobral, Patricia Lyfoung, Philippe Ogaki, Jenny, Dara, Alice Picard, and Magali Paillat. The heroes are descendants of mythological gods and they must battle an ancient evil that has returned to earth after being banished for a millennia. They are: Yuko, 14, of Japan; Parvati, 12, of India; Amir, 11, of Egypt; Abigail, 15, of Germany; Miguel, 13, of Mexico; and Neo, 16, of Greece. This multi-cultural conglomeration of characters are facing the challenge of their life—can they save the world? Or has Evil finally won? While this series has its funny moments, it's a real super-hero series with lots of super action and super-heroes we're sure you'll love!

Obviously, Lincoln and Clyde aren't the only ones who love super-heroes, as seen in this super-special SUPER SPECIAL. Super-heroes are everywhere you look these days, but we hope you'll enjoy the off-beat, fun, and original super-heroes available from Papercutz, as well as the continuing misadventures of super-hero fans such as Lincoln Loud and Clyde McBride in THE LOUD HOUSE graphic novels from Papercutz.

Thanks, Jim

STAY IN TOUCH!

EMAIL: salicrup@papercutz.com
WEB: papercutz.com
TWITTER: @papercutzgn
INSTAGRAM: @papercutzgn
FACEBOOK: PAPERCUTZGRAPHICNOVELS

Go to papercutz.com and sign up for the free Papercutz e-newsletter!